BLACK DOG

BOOKS BY STUART WOODS

FICTION

*Black Dog**
*A Safe House**
*Criminal Mischief**
*Foul Play**
*Class Act**
*Double Jeopardy**
*Hush-Hush**
*Shakeup**
*Choppy Water**
*Hit List**
*Treason**
*Stealth**
*Contraband**
*Wild Card**
*A Delicate Touch**
*Desperate Measures**
*Turbulence**
*Shoot First**
*Unbound**
*Quick & Dirty**
*Indecent Exposure**
*Fast & Loose**
*Below the Belt**
*Sex, Lies & Serious Money**
*Dishonorable Intentions**
*Family Jewels**
*Scandalous Behavior**
*Foreign Affairs**
*Naked Greed**
*Hot Pursuit**
*Insatiable Appetites**
*Paris Match**
*Cut and Thrust**
*Carnal Curiosity**
*Standup Guy**
*Doing Hard Time**
*Unintended Consequences**
*Collateral Damage**
*Severe Clear**
*Unnatural Acts**
*D.C. Dead**
*Son of Stone**
*Bel-Air Dead**
*Strategic Moves**
Santa Fe Edge†
*Lucid Intervals**
*Kisser**
Hothouse Orchid‡
*Loitering with Intent**
Mounting Fears§
*Hot Mahogany**
Santa Fe Dead†
Beverly Hills Dead
*Shoot Him If He Runs**
*Fresh Disasters**
Short Straw†
*Dark Harbor**
Iron Orchid‡
*Two Dollar Bill**
The Prince of Beverly Hills
*Reckless Abandon**
Capital Crimes§
*Dirty Work**
Blood Orchid‡
*The Short Forever**
Orchid Blues‡

*Cold Paradise**
*L.A. Dead**
The Run§
*Worst Fears Realized**
Orchid Beach‡
*Swimming to Catalina**
*Dead in the Water**
*Dirt**
Choke
Imperfect Strangers
Heat
Dead Eyes
L.A. Times
Santa Fe Rules†
*New York Dead**
Palindrome
Grass Roots§
White Cargo
Deep Lie§
Under the Lake
Run Before the Wind§
Chiefs§

COAUTHORED BOOKS

*Jackpot*** (with Bryon Quertermous)
*Bombshell*** (with Parnell Hall)
*Skin Game*** (with Parnell Hall)
*The Money Shot*** (with Parnell Hall)
Barely Legal†† (with Parnell Hall)
*Smooth Operator*** (with Parnell Hall)

AUTOBIOGRAPHY

An Extravagant Life

TRAVEL

A Romantic's Guide to the Country Inns of Britain and Ireland (1979)

MEMOIR

Blue Water, Green Skipper

*A Stone Barrington Novel
†An Ed Eagle Novel
‡A Holly Barker Novel
§A Will Lee Novel
**A Teddy Fay Novel
††A Herbie Fisher Novel

BLACK DOG

STUART WOODS

G. P. PUTNAM'S SONS
NEW YORK

PUTNAM
— EST. 1838 —

G. P. Putnam's Sons
Publishers Since 1838
An imprint of Penguin Random House LLC
penguinrandomhouse.com

Library of Congress Cataloging-in-Publication Data

Names: Woods, Stuart, author.
Title: Black dog / Stuart Woods.
Description: New York: G. P. Putnam's Sons, 2022. |
Series: Stone Barrington; 62
Identifiers: LCCN 2022019014 (print) | LCCN 2022019015 (ebook) |
ISBN 9780593540008 (hardcover) | ISBN 9780593540015 (ebook)
Subjects: LCGFT: Novels.
Classification: LCC PS3573.O642 B53 2022 (print) |
LCC PS3573.O642 (ebook) | DDC 813/.54—dc23
LC record available at https://lccn.loc.gov/2022019014
LC ebook record available at https://lccn.loc.gov/2022019015
p. cm.

Printed in the United States of America
1 3 5 7 9 10 8 6 4 2

BLACK DOG

ONE

Stone Barrington sat at his desk in his office on the ground floor of his Turtle Bay townhouse, finishing a stack of work that his secretary, Joan Robertson, had created to keep him busy. He was a senior partner at Woodman & Weld, a prestigious firm housed nearby in the Seagram Building, on Park Avenue at Fifty-Third Street. But he preferred to work in his home office, because people didn't wander up and down the halls asking him to work on the accounts of various clients.

Joan rapped on his door and came into his office. "I have a new client for you," she said. "Don't groan and roll your eyes."

Stone stifled a groan and tried to keep his eyes straight ahead. "All right, what waif have you picked up on the street?"

"She's not a waif, she's an aunt. Mine. My mother's younger sister. Her name is Annetta Charles."

"Why isn't her name Robertson, like yours?"

"Because she had the wit to marry a very rich man named Edwin Charles."

Some switch in his frontal lobe came on. "Edwin Charles?"

"I'll wait while you try and catch up," Joan said.

"*The* Edwin Charles?"

"Welcome back to full consciousness."

Edwin Charles, Stone now remembered, had occupied an elevation at approximately the Rockefeller level of existence. He had died a few months earlier from mysterious ill health. "And how may I serve dear Mrs. Charles?"

"She's going to explain that to you," Joan said. "Shall I show her in?"

"Does she have an appointment?"

"Aunt Annetta does not make appointments. She just arrives, and people—smart people—see her immediately."

"Any advice?"

"Don't kowtow too much. She doesn't like it."

Stone stood up and put on his jacket. "Please don't keep Mrs. Charles waiting."

Joan disappeared and returned a moment later, escorting a handsome woman who appeared to be somewhere in her forties. She was perfectly dressed in the manner of New York's women of the Upper East Side, and even managed to show a bit of tasteful cleavage.

"Stone," Joan said, "this is my aunt Annetta, Mrs. Edwin Charles. Aunt Annetta," she said, "this is Mr. Stone Barrington, a senior partner of Woodman & Weld."

"How do you do?" she said to Stone.

"Very well, thank you. Will you please be seated?"

She did so, flashing a glimpse of thigh as she crossed her legs.

"How may I be of assistance to you?" Stone asked.

"I want to make a new will," she replied. As she did so, she reached into her commodious handbag, withdrew a thick document, and tossed it onto Stone's desk. It landed with a thump.

"May I ask, what firm currently represents you?" Stone asked, thumbing through it.

"A little collection of desks called Woodman & Weld," she said pleasantly. "I called my attorney, Ralph Mason, for a revision and was told that he was dead. I must say, I would have thought the firm would have notified me."

"Mr. Mason, I'm sorry to say, passed away the day before yesterday," Stone replied. "I assure you notification is on its way."

"Well, at least he had an excuse for not returning my call." She brushed away some imaginary lint from her skirt.

"I'll read this just as soon as possible," Stone said.

"It won't be as hard as you might imagine," she said. "I've no quarrel with the contents except for the one document relating to my stepson, Edwin Jr."

Stone grabbed a legal pad and unsheathed his pen. "What changes would you like to make?"

"First, excise page three: that's the page outlining my stepson's legacy."

Stone found page three, pulled it from the document, and set it aside. "Done."

"Now, I would like you to set up a trust for Eddie," she said.

"It should pay him one hundred thousand dollars a month, for my lifetime."

"For *your* lifetime?"

"Yes."

"Why your lifetime, not his?"

"It's the only way I can think of to stop him from killing me."

Stone was brought up short.

"Let me explain," she said. "Since my husband's death, I have been receiving threatening notes. I am certain they are from Eddie. He is the black dog of the family."

"You mean 'black sheep'?"

"There is no sheep in Eddie," she said. "He's all dog, all the way through, and a mean one at that."

"I see," Stone replied, although he did not. "And what happens to his bequest after your death?"

"The bequest outlined in the present will is to be paid into the trust you are creating, and he may withdraw funds from it only with the permission of the trustee."

"And who would you like the trustee to be?"

"You."

Stone blinked. "Why, may I ask?"

"I happen to know—and this is not by way of your secretary—that you have a son who received a large bequest, that you are his trustee, and that you have done a remarkably good job in that role."

"Well, I'm grateful for the praise, whatever its origin. Perhaps you could tell me a little about Edwin Charles Jr.?"

She shrugged. "Eddie is, not to put too fine a point on it, a right little shite."

"That is rather a broad description," Stone replied. "Could you be more specific?"

"His father had become sick, and instead of caring for the man, all Eddie could see was the paycheck. All he did was badger his father for more money, right on his deathbed. Eddie is selfish, to the point of caring nothing about the feelings or needs of any other person; he is cruel, unfeeling, and, at once, both priggish and piggish. He is demanding, but ungiving, foul of both tongue and temper. Now I feel that twistedness turning in my direction."

"Why don't you cut him off entirely?" Stone asked.

"Eddie may seem simply a nuisance, but there is a dangerous side to him. Full disinheritance might set that off sooner than one would like. But I want it part of the document that he is never again to enter my home or any room of any other house where I might be present. Did I mention that I want you to explain all this to him?"

"Ah, no."

"I would imagine that, being a lawyer, the first thing that entered your mind was 'What's in it for me?'"

"Actually, that was the second or third thing that entered my mind."

"Let's cut to the chase," she said. "If I approve of the way you write this document, *and* the manner in which you impart the news to Eddie, I will withdraw all my legal representation by other firms and move everything to Woodman & Weld, to be supervised by you. And before you ask, my legal expenses last year exceeded a million and a half dollars. In some years, it has been substantially more."

Stone buzzed Joan, and she appeared in the doorway. "Yes, sir?"

"Please print out our standard client representation agreement for your aunt's signature. And I will make revisions to her will, which will be slight, and you can prepare it for her signature. Please gather three witnesses."

"I like the way you work, Stone, if I may call you that. And you must call me Annetta."

"Of course, Annetta," Stone replied.

A little more than an hour later, Annetta Charles signed her new will, which included the trust for Edwin Charles Jr., and it was duly witnessed by members of Stone's household staff.

Fortified by a good lunch, Annetta Charles said her goodbyes and was escorted to her waiting car by her niece.

Joan came back a moment later. "By the way," she said, "Aunt Annetta is sixty."

TWO

The following afternoon, Joan entered Stone's office and said, "Edwin Charles Jr. is here to see you, at Aunt Annetta's suggestion."

Stone sighed, steeling himself for the task. "Send him in."

Joan ushered in a young man—shy of thirty, Stone thought—who wore a finely tailored tweed suit, handmade shoes and shirt, and a gold watch chain affixed to his waistcoat.

Joan introduced them, and they shook hands.

"Call me Eddie," the young man said. "But *nobody* calls me Junior."

"Duly noted, Eddie. I'm Stone. Please take a chair. Would you like some refreshment?"

"Perhaps a large single malt whisky over ice," he replied.

"I think, given our business, coffee might be more appropriate. After that is concluded, we can think about opening the bar."

Eddie shrugged. "Now, why has my wicked stepmother insisted I see you?"

"Mrs. Charles has created a trust fund in your name. It is called the Edwin Charles Junior—or ECJ—Trust."

Eddie frowned. "Okay. Why?"

"Mrs. Charles sees you as being profligate, and she wishes to provide for you generously. But with limitations."

"'Limitations'?" Eddie asked. "What does that mean?"

"Please wait until I have outlined the terms of your trust before asking questions."

"Okay, shoot."

"The ECJ Trust will provide you with an income of one hundred thousand dollars per month, which is meant to cover *all* your living expenses—that is, food, clothing, shelter, transportation, entertainment, and whims."

Eddie's face fell. He took a breath to speak, but Stone held up a hand.

"Not yet. I have persuaded Mrs. Charles that should you become and remain gainfully employed, the trust will also pay you an amount equal to your monthly paycheck. Such payments will begin when you have submitted proper documents substantiating your hiring and your monthly income, and end if your employment should be terminated by either you or your employer."

"What am I supposed to do?" Eddie demanded.

"I'm told that you possess a law degree from Yale, is that correct?"

"It is."

"Then I suggest that you take a bar exam cram course, then take the exam. If you pass, you will be employable as an attorney. If you fail, you will not starve, given your monthly income from the trust. Then you can study harder and take the exam again."

Eddie was crestfallen. "I've never worked a day in my life. I'm unaccustomed to it."

"After you've done it for a while, you may come to enjoy it," Stone said. "Many people do. If not, then you will simply have to live within your newfound means."

"I'll sue," Eddie said.

"On what grounds? Search your legal education for an answer."

"I'm entitled."

"Entitlement is not grounds. You are entitled only to what your stepmother says you are, and she has spoken. Incidentally, you are to pack up your personal possessions and move out of her house within seventy-two hours. I suggest a room at the Yale Club temporarily and a storage unit for your excess possessions. And, if I may put this in a Dickensian manner, you are never again to darken her door—or any other door where she is present, on pain of ending the income stream from your trust. Do you have any questions?"

Eddie thought about it and shook his head.

"Good," Stone said, handing him an envelope. "Here is your first month's check, and another to cover your immediate rehousing."

"Who is the trustee?" Eddie asked.

"I am," Stone said, "and only I. Any requests will be heard by me and not your stepmother." He pressed a button, and Joan appeared with Eddie's coat. Eddie followed her out.

"Call me a taxi," Eddie demanded sullenly.

"Okay, you're a taxi." She pushed him out the front door and locked it behind him, then she returned to Stone's office. "How'd the Black Dog take it?" she asked.

"I think he was too stunned to protest much."

"It was generous of you to add an amount equal to his income."

"Your aunt rather liked that, too. I hope we've heard the last of Eddie."

"Don't count on it," Joan said.

THREE

Stone regarded his secretary. "You noticed that you were not a witness to the signing of your aunt's will?"

"Of course."

"Do you know why?"

"I presume it was because I am an heir."

"A good presumption. Now, your aunt Annetta seemed reluctant in the extreme to chat about her stepson."

"I'm not surprised. He has caused her a great deal of pain."

"Perhaps you will enlighten me on the nature of that pain. It would be helpful if I could know what to expect from him."

"Your worst fears realized," she replied.

"Specifics, please."

"You will have noticed that, in her will, there are bequests for the rearing and education of three children."

"I did. I had supposed that Eddie was her only stepchild."

"He is. The three children are what might be called her step-grandchildren."

"I take it that Eddie is heterosexual."

"He is and, apparently, perpetually priapic."

"Ah. What else?"

"I don't think he's, clinically speaking, an alcoholic or a drug addict, but I believe that he has sampled, at least once, whatever is available in the world of consciousness-altering pharmaceuticals. His drug of choice seems to be some very expensive product of Scottish agriculture and distilling—sometimes to excess, hence the step-grandchildren."

"Would you describe him as heedless?"

"Of almost everything," Joan replied.

"What of his judgment?"

"Little, or none."

"Moral character?"

"Unknown to him."

"It sounds as if I'm going to soon hear from him with a request for further funds."

"Before the day is out is my best guess."

"I'm not going to refuse his calls, exactly, but he should never be put through to me immediately, nor should he ever be in possession of my cell phone number."

"Certainly not. Anything else, boss?"

"Yes, why did you recommend me to Aunt Annetta?"

"Because, in my judgment, the fees accruing to Woodman & Weld will far exceed whatever trouble Eddie turns out to be.

I thought it preferable to make rain, rather than to stay high and dry."

"Joan, am I ever going to want to hide from my new charge?"

"Frequently, I fear," Joan replied.

The office line rang, and Stone indicated that Joan should use his desk phone to answer it. "Woodman & Weld, the Barrington Practice." She listened for a moment, then covered the phone. "Eddie wants me to send a check for $2,200 to the phone company for the installation of four telephone lines and a superfast Internet connection to his suite at the Yale Club."

"Tell him it's time to open a bank account."

Joan did so, then hung up before he could protest. "That was good," she said. "I think we've established a baseline for saying no to Eddie."

"Next time he tries something like that, tell him to try moving to a room rather than a suite at his club. If you receive any bills for anything from him, mark the envelopes 'not at this address' and forward them to him at the Yale Club. That includes any bills from the Yale Club."

"Any further instructions?"

"Yes, if you receive calls or mail or a request for bail money that mentions Eddie as being my client, deny it. Say that Woodman & Weld has his trust fund for a client, not Eddie Jr."

"Sounds as if you want to sever all ties."

"I would if I could, but we can reduce the number of ties to as near zero as possible."

The phone rang again.

"Dino," Joan said.

"Hi, there."

"Dinner, Clarke's, seven o'clock?"

"Done." They both hung up.

Stone arrived a little late at P. J. Clarke's and found Dino at the bar, chatting with Eddie Jr.

"Ah, Stone," Dino said. "I've just met your new client."

"And who might that be?" Stone asked.

"This guy," Dino said, pointing.

Stone turned to Eddie. "Who are you?"

Eddie's jaw dropped. "It's me, Eddie."

"Eddie who?"

"Edwin Charles Jr."

"I have no such client," Stone replied. "Dino, I think this guy is running a scam. Isn't that illegal in New York?"

"You want me to run him in?"

"I'll leave that judgment to you."

"Now wait a minute," Eddie said, tugging at Stone's sleeve.

Stone pointed at his sleeve. "I believe that action constitutes assault," he said to Dino.

"You want me to bust him?"

"I'll be content if he just dematerializes."

Dino took a small radio from an inside pocket. "Charlie?"

"Yes, Commissioner?"

"There's a guy in here at the bar harassing Mr. Barrington. I'd like for him to go away."

Eddie witnessed this exchange wide-eyed. Then, before he could speak, a uniformed patrolman entered the bar and walked over. "Is this the guy?" he asked, pointing to Stone.

"No, that's Barrington."

"Sorry, Mr. Barrington," the man said with a little salute.

"This is the guy," Dino said, pointing at Eddie, who had started to walk backward.

"Sorry for the intrusion," he said, then turned and fled.

"Thank you, Charlie," Dino said. "Please see that he doesn't make any U-turns."

FOUR

Stone and Dino were polishing off their steaks when Stone's cell phone rang. He answered it automatically. "Hello?"

"Why did you act as if you don't know me?" Eddie Jr. asked.

"Hello? Hello?"

"It's me, Eddie."

"Hello? There's nobody here," he said to Dino, then hung up. "How the hell did he get my cell number?"

"There are ways," Dino said. "You employ them all the time. Don't worry, he'll call again, and you can ignore the call."

Stone took out his cell phone and turned it completely off.

"Now he'll go straight to voice mail," Stone said.

"Good thinking."

They ordered cheesecake and were nearly finished when Eddie Jr. appeared at their table and stood there, glaring at Stone. "Well?"

"Did you hear something?" Stone asked Dino. He took a sip of his red wine and set it down near the edge of the table. Then he reached over, took Dino's half-full glass, and poured it into his own.

"Hey!" Dino said, waving at a waiter for two more glasses.

Stone reached for a paper napkin on the table and used his forearm to tip the wineglass over. The wine struck Eddie's leg at about the knee and ran down his tan trouser leg.

Eddie made a loud noise and jumped backward into the waiter who was carrying two more glasses of wine, which spilled onto Eddie, too.

"Hey, watch it!" Dino said. "You're making a mess!"

Eddie was grabbing paper napkins and dabbing at his trousers.

"You did that on purpose!" he said to Stone.

"I didn't do anything. You backed into the waiter. If you'll stand still for a minute, I'll order two more glasses, and you can try to spill those."

Dino made a shooing motion with his hands. "Get out, or I'll have you arrested for disturbing the peace."

The headwaiter came over, waving a cloth napkin at Eddie. Then he took Eddie by the elbow and led him away. He came back after a moment. "I'm sorry about the nuisance," he said. "Every time that guy comes in here, he starts something."

"I shouldn't think you'd want him back in your restaurant," Stone said.

"I'll eighty-six the guy," the maître d' said. "You won't see him again in here." He went back to his desk to receive another party.

"I wish we could get him eighty-sixed from Manhattan," Stone said.

"Is Rikers Island far enough away?" Dino asked, referring to the city jail facility.

"Almost," Stone said. "Can you get him arrested in New Jersey?"

"Who is that guy?" Dino asked.

"His stepmother, Annetta Charles, widow of the recently deceased Edwin Charles, is a new client of mine. She's pretty much fenced him off from her presence."

"Yeah? Edwin Charles was very rich, wasn't he?"

"He was. Now his widow is. She's quite a number. Have you seen her?"

"I think on Page Six." Meaning the gossip column in the *New York Post.*

"She's sixty and looks forty."

"Watch out," Dino said.

"Don't worry, the bar association of New York has fenced her off from me. Legal ethics require me not to diddle my clients."

"Has that ever stopped you before?"

"Always," Stone replied.

"It's a pity the bar association can't protect you from—What's-his-name?"

"Eddie Jr. I'm counting on the NYPD for that assistance."

"I don't think a charge of disturbing the peace will keep

him far enough away," Dino said. "Dream up something with some jail time attached, and I'll see what I can do."

"I guess that assault on my jacket sleeve wasn't enough, huh?"

"Get him to assault you with something in his hand, like a baseball bat."

"I'm not sure I would survive that sort of assault."

"Okay. How about a closed fist?"

"I think he's too much of a coward to try that," Stone replied. "Joan says he's devoid of any moral character, so I'm sure he'll think of something we can nail him for."

"Your police department remains at your beck and call," Dino said.

FIVE

Stone had breakfast in bed, as always, then showered, shaved, dressed, and went downstairs to his home office.

Joan came in from her office. "Have you called a press conference for this morning?"

"Press conference? Me? What about?"

"My very question," Joan replied.

"What are you talking about, Joan?"

"There's a little knot of seedy-looking people with press badges gathered on our doorstep, and they seem to be waiting to be spoken to."

"Thank God I don't have a hangover," Stone said, "or I wouldn't be able to gather myself to address them."

"Well, since you don't have a hangover, why don't you go outside and disperse them."

"Because I pay you for that sort of chore."

"I tried speaking to them, but they ignored me."

Stone got up from his desk, put on his jacket, and walked outside. "Disperse!" he said to the gathering, making shooing motions. They ignored him and continued to chat among themselves.

"Good morning, ladies and gentlemen," a voice behind Stone said. They all snapped to something like attention.

Stone turned to find Eddie Jr. standing on an upturned flowerpot, from which the flowers had been cast aside.

"I suppose you're wondering why I've called you all together," Eddie said. They became reverently silent.

"Put that flowerpot back where you found it," Stone said to him, "and put the flowers back into it."

"After I've addressed the press," Eddie said.

"Address them somewhere else, or I'll have the police haul them all away, you included."

"Don't be ridiculous," Eddie said.

"Joan," Stone said to her. "Call the police and ask them to haul this crowd away."

"On what grounds?" she asked, having joined him outside.

"Making a public nuisance," Stone replied.

"I'm afraid they're standing on a public sidewalk. They can do anything they like there, including making a public nuisance of themselves."

"Have you recently graduated from law school and passed the bar?" he asked her.

"No, but someone has," she replied, nodding at Eddie Jr.

"Ladies and gentlemen," Eddie said, "I have recently taken

and passed the bar exam and am now an attorney-at-law, licensed to practice in New York State."

"Oh, come on, Eddie!" a reporter shouted.

"I refer you to page twenty-four of this morning's *Daily News*," Eddie said, "where you will find my name on the long list of those who passed the bar exam." He handed them the newspaper, and they passed it around for everyone to see.

"I suggested that to you only yesterday," Stone said. "Did you bribe someone to add your name to the list?"

"I took the exam ten days ago," Eddie said, "in the expectation of someone suggesting that I might seek employment in a law firm. I'm smarter than you think I am, Mr. Barrington. They're just getting around to announcing it." Eddie took an envelope from his inside coat pocket and handed it to Stone. "Here is my curriculum vitae and particulars. I wish to be employed by Woodman & Weld."

Stone handed it back to him. "Personnel is just around the corner in the Seagram Building. You may submit your application there. Please give me time to call them and instruct them to deny your application before you submit it."

"That is highly prejudicial," Eddie said. He turned back to the crowd. "Do you see how I'm being treated? I am a graduate of Yale University and Yale Law School, and I am fully qualified for employment as an attorney."

"You have no experience to qualify you," Stone said. "Now, please go away."

"I worked at Woodman & Weld for four summers as an intern," Eddie said.

"In what department?" Stone demanded.

"In eight departments, two a summer. Check with Mr. Grady, the director of personnel."

Stone leaned over near Joan's ear. "Call Grady and check that out," he whispered.

Joan disappeared into the office. She returned shortly. "He's not lying," she said.

"Well?" Eddie demanded.

"You are temperamentally unsuited to work at Woodman & Weld," Stone said to him.

"Says who?"

"Says a senior partner of the firm. Now get out of here and take this passel of ink-stained wretches with you." Stone took Joan's arm and propelled her back into the office. "Call Grady and tell him that Edwin Charles Jr. is temperamentally unsuited for employment at Woodman & Weld."

"Yes, sir."

Stone went back into his office, hung up his jacket, and addressed the little pile of mail and messages on his desk.

"Excuse me, Stone," Joan said. "Mr. Grady would like to speak with you."

"Did you tell him what I said?"

"Yes, that's why he wants to speak with you."

Stone picked up the phone and pushed a button. "Ellis, it's Stone Barrington. What can I do for you?"

"Stone, you can explain to me why you don't want Eddie Charles to work at Woodman & Weld."

"Are you telling me that you do?" Stone asked, amazed.

"Why? I've heard he's bright, hardworking, and has a prodigious memory for cases. He's a walking, talking Lexis," Grady said, referring to the legal reference service.

Stone was feeling cornered now, but he had a way out. "Ellis, are you acquainted with Eddie's stepmother, Annetta Charles?"

"I haven't met her, but I certainly know who she is."

"Are you aware that, yesterday, she became a client of the firm, moving all her legal work to us?"

"I hadn't heard that, but it's certainly good news."

"Then you are not aware that she made it a condition of being our client that her stepson, Eddie, would have nothing whatever to do with the firm?" This was an exaggeration, but Stone was now desperate.

"I was not aware of that."

"Then see that any application of Eddie Jr. to the firm is rejected out of hand."

"As you wish," Grady said, then hung up.

"You think that will do it?" Stone asked Joan.

"Maybe," Joan said.

SIX

Joan buzzed Stone after lunch. "Bill Eggers for you on one." Eggers was the managing partner of Woodman & Weld who had brought Stone aboard not long after he left the NYPD.

Stone picked up the phone. "Good morning, Bill."

"Good morning, Stone." He paused.

"What can I do for you?"

"Stone, I try not to meddle in the day-to-day working of our various departments, but a few minutes ago I got a call from Ellis Grady, our recently appointed personnel director. It seems that you have, in effect, blackballed a job applicant, and one that Ellis feels is well qualified. Why did you do that?"

"Bill, did Ellis tell you the applicant's name?"

"One Edward Charles, I believe."

"That is incorrect. His name is Edwin Charles Jr. Does that ring a bell?"

"Would he, in some way, be related to Edwin Charles, our new client?"

"No, Bill. That Mr. Charles was deceased about four months ago."

"Then his estate is our client?"

"No, Bill. His widow, Annetta Charles, is our client."

"That's good, isn't it?"

"I believe so. And I'm surprised that I have not received a congratulatory phone call from you, for making such a large amount of rain."

"How much rain are we talking about?"

"Buckets full. Her annual legal expenditures have been running in excess of a million dollars."

"Stone, allow me to congratulate you, although belatedly, for bringing in some important new business."

"Thank you, Bill, it's kind of you to mention it."

"Tell me, is Edwin Charles Jr. related to our new client?"

"He is her despised stepson."

"Define 'despised.'"

"Hated in the extreme, so much so that she has declared a sort of personal temporary restraining order, covering anywhere she might choose to be."

"Surely, Stone, that would not include the offices of the law firm that represents her."

"Surely, Bill, it would. She made no exceptions in her TRO for the premises of Woodman & Weld."

"Well, that is unfortunate."

"If you should have the opportunity to meet and get to know Eddie Jr., you may wish to reconsider your statement."

"Is our Ellis Grady cognizant of Mrs. Charles's feelings toward her stepson?"

"Ellis appears to be information-resistant where Eddie Jr. is concerned."

"How odd."

"Very. Mr. Grady is fairly new to us, isn't he?"

"He joined us about three months ago, I believe."

"It would be interesting to have a look at his application, I think."

"I'll call you back," Eggers said.

Joan rapped on Stone's door. He waved her to a seat. She looked around. "What's going on?"

"I'm endeavoring to construct a bomb under Junior's application for employment at Woodman & Weld."

"Oh."

"What are your earliest memories of your cousin, Eddie Jr.?" Stone asked.

"Well, as a boy he liked abusing small animals, like cats, but not limited to them. And he loved setting things on fire."

The phone rang and Joan answered it. "Woodman & Weld. Hold, please." She covered the phone. "Bill Eggers for you."

Stone picked up his phone. "Yes, Bill?"

"Stone, thank you for your suggestion. I have examined Mr. Grady's file, including his employment application, and have found it to include a fulsome letter of recommendation of Mr.

Grady's skills and character from Edwin Charles Sr., dated a week before he died. The original envelope was attached, and it was postmarked two weeks *after* Mr. Charles expired."

"Aha," Stone replied. "I had assumed something of the sort."

"Mr. Grady is, as we speak, cleaning out his desk, under the watchful eyes of two of our security guards, who are examining everything he takes with him. He will be leaving our employ in exactly, let's see . . . seven minutes. My secretary is typing up a letter to Mr. Charles Jr., care of the Yale Club, denying him employment, any earlier acceptance notwithstanding, and with our best wishes. Ads will appear ASAP in appropriate publications, advertising for a new personnel manager."

"Then, in my view," Stone said, "all is right with the world. Thank you again for your congratulatory call." He hung up. "Joan, please keep on the lookout for other Eddie Jr. transgressions, which we will head off at the pass whenever possible. And if not, then at Boot Hill."

"Yes, sir," Joan said, smiling broadly.

SEVEN

As Stone was preparing to leave his office for the day, Joan came in looking flustered. "What's wrong?" he asked.

"I've just had Eddie Jr. on the phone for half an hour, berating me for having him fired. Apparently, he got back to the Yale Club and found your letter, which I had hand delivered, waiting for him."

"Were you rude to him?"

"No."

"Why not? You had every right to be, after he began blaming you for him getting canned for bribing a department head to get favorable treatment."

"I just couldn't bring myself to yell at him."

"Who do you expect to do the yelling?" Stone asked.

"You."

"Me? I've already told you that I don't want to speak to him."

"You just don't understand how hard it is to deal with him."

"All right, the next time he shows up here, I'll see him."

"Oh, thank you. He's in my office. I'll send him right in."

Before Stone could react, he found Eddie Charles Jr. in his office, berating him.

"Stop!" Stone shouted, holding up both hands.

Eddie continued unabated.

"Stop, or I'll call the police and have you arrested!"

"I can't believe you had me fired. I demand you give me access to my money. It's MINE and I have a lawful right to it. I can't believe my own lawyer is withholding funds. That's illegal!" he whined.

"Sit down," Stone said, hoping a change of position might interrupt the flow of invective.

Eddie sat down.

"Now," Stone said, "I'm going to explain some things to you, and if you interrupt me, you'll spend the night in jail. Is that what you want?"

"No."

"All right. First, I am not now, nor have I ever been, your lawyer. I am your stepmother's lawyer and that of the trust that pays you each month. Do you understand that?"

"I guess."

"Then stop telling people—and me—that I am your lawyer."

"Oh, all right. Who's my lawyer?"

"Google 'lawyers' and pick one. And confine your complaints about your life to him or her."

"You told me to get a job, I don't understand why you would get me fired on my first day."

"How much did you pay Ellis Grady to hire you?"

Eddie stared at the floor. "Ten—"

"Eddie . . . !"

"Twenty-five thousand dollars."

"Well, now he's been fired, too."

"Will I get my money back?"

"You'd better speak to Ellis Grady about that. My guess is, he's already lost it at the track."

"How did you know he was . . ."

"How did *you* know? I guessed that he had to be in deep debt before he would take money from a job applicant. He may very well lose his law license."

"He's not a lawyer," Eddie pointed out.

"Well, the bar association can breathe easier now. Who did you pay to say that you'd passed the bar?"

"I didn't do that! I took that cram course weeks before you suggested it, and I knew the answer to almost every question they asked."

"Who gave you the questions before the exam?"

"Listen, you don't know how smart I am! I have a photographic memory, and I can remember anything I see or read!"

"Oh, yeah? Then how is it you can't remember that I'm not your attorney?"

"Well, my memory is, sometimes, ah, a little dicey."

"A lot of the time it appears to fail completely."

"That, too."

"Do you have a police record, Eddie?"

"No! They've never been able to prove a thing!"

Stone laughed in spite of himself. "You can't go on working on that premise, Eddie. One of these days, they'll have the proof handy, and you'll find yourself sharing a cell with a big guy who likes to beat up on rich pretty boys like you."

"I've met that guy once," Eddie said disconsolately.

"Well, if you meet him again in prison, you're a sitting duck."

"Why are you saying these terrible things to me?"

"I'm just trying to get you to confront reality for once in your life."

"I confront it every day, and I don't like it!"

"Trust me, Eddie, that's not going to change. The only thing that can change is your ability to deal with it. You should work on that."

Eddie nodded. "I know."

"Well, then. Take your newfound knowledge of yourself and get thee to the Yale Club. I'm surprised they haven't kicked you out yet."

"Well, I did have one conversation with the house committee, but I talked my way out of it."

"They're onto you, then. Have they checked your Yale credentials yet?"

"Yes, and they found that I had a 3.9 GPA."

"I'm sure that impressed them, and they'll be further impressed if your conduct doesn't bring you to their attention again."

"I understand."

"If that's true, then God has not put me on Earth for nothing."

"God put you on Earth?"

"So to speak," Stone said. "Now, go and do good works. Everybody will notice, and you'll get along better in the world."

"Good work doesn't go as far as good money does. You're naïve, Stone, if you don't see that!"

"Maybe," Stone said.

Joan appeared in the door. "Time to go, Eddie," she said. He followed her like a puppy, then she came back to Stone's office. "I'm sorry about that. I'll try to see it doesn't happen again."

"Double-lock the door," Stone said.

EIGHT

Stone called Mike Freeman, CEO of Strategic Services, one of the nation's largest security firms, on whose board Stone sat.

"Hey, Stone."

"Afternoon, Mike. I'd like you to run a deep check on somebody."

"Who might that be?"

"One Edwin Charles Jr."

"Son of the late Edwin Charles Sr.?"

"One and the same."

"What do you want to know?"

"Everything there is to know. I keep getting surprised."

"I can do that. Give me a day."

"Great. And bill the Edwin Charles Junior Trust. I'm his trustee." Stone had a thought. "Let's do the rest of the family, too—Edwin Charles Sr. and Annetta Charles, his widow."

"New business, I hear."

"Gotta oil the wheels, don't we?"

"You betcha. Let's have lunch tomorrow. I should have something by then. The Grill, at one?"

"See you there."

Joan peered from around the corner. "You're running checks on members of my family, dead and alive?"

"I am. I forgot to add your name to the list," Stone replied.

"What could you possibly want to know about us?"

"Everything. I can't get much out of you."

"I've answered every question you asked me."

"What about the ones I didn't ask you? Tell me about those."

Joan rolled her eyes. "I could have saved you the money."

"It's Eddie's trust's money," Stone said. "I'm entitled to know what and whom I'm dealing with."

"I thought I was helping."

"And yet, I keep getting smacked in the kisser by surprises! That's nerve-racking, don't you understand that?"

"It's nerve-racking to get the third degree from you, too."

"What have you got to hide?"

"I'm sure Mike Freeman will come up with something."

"Did you do time for embezzlement of your employer's funds?"

"No! Of course not!"

"Then you've got nothing to worry about, have you? Or have you? Best to tell me now."

"I don't like telling on people."

"Then meet some people who don't have anything to be told about them."

"I'm stuck with the ones I've got," she said. Then she went back to her desk, while Stone wondered what she was talking about.

Stone met Mike Freeman the following day for lunch. They each ordered a drink and lunch, then Mike opened his briefcase and set a file folder on the table. "Ready?"

Stone took a deep breath and exhaled. "Hit me."

"Okay, let's start with some good news."

Stone looked surprised. "I didn't think there would be any."

"Eddie Jr.'s academic record stands up. He was a smart kid who worked hard at his studies, and he left Groton, Yale, and Yale Law School in good order. His appearance on the bar exam list of passes is legit, too."

"I'm stunned!" Stone said. "How'd he get to be such a weasel?"

"An indulgent papa," Mike said. "He was good in school and got a zero in behavior."

"Any reason why?"

"Excess in just about everything—girls, booze, gambling, you name it."

"Does he have a record?"

"Nope, his sheet is clean."

"That doesn't make sense."

"Do you know a lawyer named Jacob Marvin?"

"Jake the Snake? Doesn't everybody?"

"Well, Jake, as you well know, was reputed, in his day, to be very adept at moving cash from pocket to palm, and Eddie Sr. had him on retainer, for the personal use of Eddie Jr."

"That explains a lot," Stone said.

"Every time Junior got busted, Jake made it all go away. Thus, Junior's clean slate."

"Is there a list somewhere of what he was charged with?"

"He was never charged. Jake was that quick."

"Well, I can't confront the kid with missing court appearances, because there weren't any?"

"You're very quick. That's about all there is to tell about Junior. You want to hear about the rest of the family?"

Lunch came and was served. "Okay," Stone said, around a chunk of Dover sole.

"Eddie Sr., in addition to running his hedge fund, was banking three or four loan sharks."

"Well, that's a cash-rich business, if you can hide the proceeds."

"The loan sharks were wiring Eddie's share of the vigorish straight into a Caymans bank account. He also kept a large safety-deposit box at a bank near his office where bundles of the green stuff were stowed, until Eddie or Annetta, as she likes to be called now, could think of something to spend it on."

"My goodness!"

"Wait until I tell you about his wife, or Apple Annie, as she was known in the bordello where she spent a few years in a bedroom. Then she met Eddie."

"He was a customer?"

"Her best regular. She apparently had a peculiar talent for satisfying his particular needs. With Eddie's assistance, she moved up to management."

"Holy shit! The society grande dame!"

"She never went near the premises. She confined herself to hiring and firing and the books—plus making regular trips to the safety-deposit box."

"And what happened to all this when Eddie Sr. fell off the perch?"

"She was in complete control of everything, and she kept it all. Probate was unnecessary."

"How much?"

"Nobody knows for sure, but a survey of his, later her, assets suggests tens of millions annually, and even after the big spending, better than a hundred mil stashed away."

"I think I'll have some dessert, while I try to digest this," Stone said.

NINE

Stone got back to his office and put the file folders on the Charleses into his safe.

Joan came in. "So, now do you know everything there is to know about my family?"

"The files are in my safe. If you know everything, it won't hurt you to read them, but if you know nothing, my advice is to let them lie."

"Aunt Annetta just called. She wants you to come and see her."

"When does she want me to come?"

"Ten minutes ago."

"Okay, alert Fred."

"He's waiting in the garage."

"All right," he said, getting back into his jacket. "I'll be back when I'm back."

"Nicely put."

Stone got out of the car a door or two off Fifth Avenue in the Sixties. It was not an apartment building but a house. Stone rang the bell, and a moment later, a uniformed butler let him into a large, marbled foyer. "Good afternoon, Mr. Barrington. You are expected. Elevator or stairs?"

"Elevator," Stone said.

The butler showed him into the car and pressed eight. A moment later, he was in another foyer, and a uniformed maid greeted him and led him to the living room, which featured an expansive view of Central Park through broad windows. He was alone in the room. After taking in the view, he took one of the chairs in front of the fireplace, where logs crackled.

Another ten minutes passed before he heard the tap of high heels on marble, and Annetta Charles swept into the room, wearing a tightly fitting tailored tweed suit. "Good afternoon, Stone," she said, shaking his hand and giving him a momentary glimpse at what the suit had been designed to display. "Take a seat." She indicated the sofa and sat there, too.

"Thank you, Annetta," he replied and sat down.

"I understand that you are interested in the background of my family."

"Yes, but no more than of any other new client."

"You like to know whom you're dealing with, do you?"

"Doesn't everybody?"

"I think you'll find that we are pretty much run-of-the-mill, among wealthy Upper East Siders."

Stone was amused that she had started with a lie but tried not to show it.

"Edwin was a product of Greenwich, Yale, and MIT," she said. "I am a product of Miss Porter's School and a finishing school in Switzerland."

Stone nodded, as if all that were to be expected.

"What more would you like to know?" she asked.

"Whatever you'd like to tell me; no more."

She turned toward him, breasts first, and rested a hand on his thigh. "Your reputation with women precedes you," Annetta said, stroking the thigh.

"I wasn't aware that I had such a reputation," Stone replied, though he was.

"Do you appreciate directness in a woman?" she asked.

He placed a hand on her hand, to stop its progress. "To an extent," he said. "Within the limitations of the code of ethics of the New York State Bar Association."

"Does the bar association look down on intimacy?"

"It discourages too much intimacy between attorney and client and bans carnal relationships."

"Carnal," she said, licking her lips. "Such an attractive word. Do you think we could overlook their rule for, say, an afternoon?"

"Not until we have fundamentally changed the nature of our current relationship."

"Then what can we do?"

"Anything that I can explain to my board of partners at Woodman & Weld without blushing."

"Lie to them," she said, reaching for his zipper.

"I find lying to be a bad practice," Stone said, "that becomes worse with time."

"Well, why don't you just sit there and contemplate the rules, while I take a tour of your body. And at least one part of it appears to be growing."

"How could it not," Stone asked, "in such inviting circumstances?" He rezipped. "But I think I should keep it in check, in our present circumstances."

"You appear to be trying to get yourself fired," she said.

"That would be unfortunate for both of us," Stone replied. "I would lose a valued client, and you would lose the best legal representation available."

"Oh?" She squeezed.

Stone played his final card. "And you would have to deal with Eddie Jr. again."

Her face fell, and she pushed away from him on the sofa. "I won't ask how he's doing, because I don't want to know."

"I think that's wise," Stone said.

She stood up and brushed away imaginary wrinkles on her skirt. "Well, thank you for coming, Stone. Please continue to keep me in the dark about Junior."

"Certainly," Stone said, shaking her hand. "And good afternoon to you."

He made his way out of the living room and down in the elevator without encountering either the maid or the butler. He left the Charles residence and got into the car, breaking a light sweat in his haste. He rode downtown trying to make his breathing regular and his thoughts somewhere other than Annetta Charles's sofa. He reflected that Dino was right. He had been too long without a woman, and resisting Annetta's advances had been difficult to do.

TEN

Stone got back to his office and poured himself a Knob Creek, something he did not often do when alone in the afternoon. His breathing had returned to normal. Joan seemed to be elsewhere.

He sat down and his thoughts were irresistibly drawn to what might have happened on Annetta's sofa if he had not managed to preserve his virtue. He was able to put her aside when he remembered that Joan had warned him that Annetta was sixty, not forty. He reflected that he had never had carnal relations with someone so much older than he, not that he was opposed to the idea, in principle. He had the very strong feeling that if he had followed her down the garden path that she would, after that, have had more influence on his actions than he wished her to have. There was a noise and he jumped, spilling some of his drink on his desk.

"I'm sorry to have startled you," Joan said. "I was doing some filing in the back room and didn't hear you come in."

"That's quite all right." Here she comes, he thought.

"So, how did you and Annetta get along?"

"Passably," he said. "When I brought up the subject of Eddie Jr. she remembered that she had something else to do."

"What was she wearing?" Joan asked.

"A tweed suit with . . . What kind of a question is that?"

"Street clothes or, ah, something more comfortable?"

"What are you getting at, Joan?"

"I'm just wondering what Aunt Annetta might have been getting at."

"What?"

"She has a reputation for getting at things with dispatch."

"I wasn't there long enough to find out."

"I read the files of the Charleses while you were gone."

"And . . . ?"

"And I found them illuminating, but not surprising."

"Which parts did you find illuminating?"

"The parts about Edwin's sources of income and Aunt Annetta's, ah, career path. Nothing about Eddie Jr. would be illuminating or surprise me."

"And you think Annetta's 'career path' might have affected her behavior today?"

"I read somewhere once—maybe Kinsey—that the chief reason that prostitutes chose their trade was, not money, but because they enjoyed the sex."

"I have little experience of prostitutes, so I can't argue with that. But it sounds like something written by a man, not a woman."

Joan laughed. "It does, doesn't it?" The phone rang and she answered it. "Woodman & Weld, the Barrington Practice." She listened for a moment, then held out the phone to Stone. "It's Annetta's butler. He wants to speak to you, and he sounds odd."

"Odd how?"

"Ask him."

"This is Stone Barrington. Yes, Geoffrey, what is it?" He listened for a moment. "Now calm down, Geoffrey. There are some things you have to do. Please listen to me. First of all, you must note the time, then call 911 and tell them you want to report a death. Then you must tell the staff to stay out of the upstairs sitting room, and neither you nor they must touch anything in the room. Do you understand?" He listened. "Please tell that to the police when they arrive. I'll be there as soon as I can." He hung up and got into his jacket.

"That sounded alarming," Joan said.

"It was alarming. Geoffrey says that a staff member found Annetta dead, apparently of a gunshot."

"Damn it. Did the butler do it?"

"That remains to be seen."

"You should call Dino," Joan said.

"I'll call him on the way. Get Fred saddled up." He glanced at his wristwatch. "Please note that the call came in about 3:40 PM."

Stone hurried for the garage. As soon as they were on their way, Stone called Dino.

"Bacchetti."

"It's Stone. Do you remember Annetta Charles?"

"Yeah, she's the widow of Edwin Charles, and she's your new client."

"Not anymore. I just had a call from her butler, saying that she's dead, apparent gunshot wound."

"Did you call 911?"

"I instructed him to. Will you see that a reliable detective gets assigned to this? One who won't screw everything up?"

"I'm afraid you'll catch whoever is hanging around the precinct. My own order."

"Swell. Now I'll have to deal with one of those sorry timeservers that are rife on your police force."

"You? Why do you have to deal with anybody?"

"I may have been the last person to see her alive."

"Really."

"Except for her killer, of course."

"Of course," Dino said. "Good luck, pal." He hung up.

ELEVEN

Fred found an actual, legal parking spot a couple of doors from the Charles mansion. Also parked out front were two police cars: a cruiser with its lights flashing and an unmarked sedan with a police shield on the sun visor. Stone walked up the front steps, reached into his pocket, and withdrew the wallet that contained his police shield, getting it ready to display.

A cop stood at the door, ready to stop anyone who tried to enter. Stone showed him the badge. "I want to talk to the detective in charge."

The cop peered at the badge. "That's a retirement badge."

"You're very observant," Stone said. "I'll mention it to the commissioner when he gets here."

"The commissioner is coming to a murder scene?"

"I'd like to speak to the detective in charge," Stone repeated, brushing past the officer and ducking under the police tape.

"Everybody's on the eighth floor," the cop called after him.

Stone waved his thanks without looking back. Then he got into the elevator and pressed eight. The doors opened, and he had to duck under more tape. There were a couple of uniforms and a couple of suits in the room. The younger suit walked over to him and blocked his path. "This is a crime scene, pal. Let's see some ID."

Stone pointed at the badge on his lapel. "Will that do you?"

"What's your business here?"

Stone looked him up and down, not uncritically. "I'd like to speak to the detective in charge," he said.

The young detective took a breath, but the older cop, who was sitting on a sofa, interrupted. "Mr. Barrington, I presume."

"That's right."

"I'm Dan Casey. What can I do for you?" He waved Stone to a seat.

Stone sat down on the sofa. "I thought I might be of help to you."

"How?"

"Well, I might be the last person to have seen her alive. Except for her killer."

"Ah, well, then tell me all about it."

"Mrs. Charles called my office when I was out and spoke to my secretary, who gave me the message."

"What was the message?"

"Mrs. Charles wanted to see me at her home."

"When?"

"Pronto. Mrs. Charles didn't make appointments. She was

accustomed to people doing her bidding; she didn't do theirs. I came right over."

"What time did you arrive?"

"A little after three o'clock, I believe."

"And what was the subject of the meeting?"

"I represent Mrs. Charles and the trust that pays her stepson, Edwin Jr., an income."

"And what did you discuss?"

"Come on, Dan, you know all about attorney-client privilege. You know I can't discuss the content of our discussion. Suffice it to say that we discussed matters of a legal nature."

"How long did you discuss them?"

"Perhaps fifteen minutes."

"That's a pretty short discussion of legal matters. Did you fuck her?"

"I did not. That would have been a violation of the code of ethics of the New York State Bar Association."

"Did you fuck her anyway?"

"Asked and answered."

"Stop dodging my questions."

"Stop wasting my time," Stone said.

"Are you carrying a gun?"

"Not today, but I sometimes do. I'm licensed for concealed carry."

"What is the caliber of your gun?"

"I own several: .45, 9mm, .40, and .380."

"Why so many?"

"I like the right tool for the work at hand. What was she shot with?"

"A .38."

"I haven't owned or carried one since I got out of the academy and sold it to a fellow student."

"Who might that have been?"

"It was a fellow called Dino Bacchetti."

"How convenient."

"It might have been convenient when the sale occurred, twenty years ago."

"Do you expect me to believe that story?"

"I don't give a damn whether you believe it or not. Do you have any more questions? If not, I'll get out of your way."

"What time did you leave?"

"The police academy?"

"This house. Today."

"About three-twenty-five."

"Anybody see you go?"

"No. I saw a butler and a maid when I arrived, but they weren't around when I left. I took the elevator down and walked out the front door. My driver can confirm what time I got into the car."

"How did you know about the shooting?"

"The butler called me about three-forty. He was shaky."

"Why you?"

"You'll have to ask him. I told him to call 911, and he said he would."

"He did. Do you represent Mrs. Charles's estate?"

"Her will names me as her executor, so yes. I represent her husband's estate, too."

"So your firm won't lose the business?"

"Not if it keeps her executor and her heir happy."

"I assume the heir is her son."

"Stepson, and you can assume what you like, but I can't comment on that right now."

"That account must represent a nice piece of change for Woodman & Weld."

"We've only been representing her for a few days, but I expect that would be true, eventually."

"I'm told that she was paying her former lawyers better than a million a year."

"I've heard that rumor, too. You'll have to confirm it with her former lawyers."

Stone heard the elevator doors open and heels clicking on the parquet floor. He turned to see Dino looking around. "Where's the body?" he asked.

"Behind the other sofa, Commissioner," Casey said. "Two in the back of the head. I'm guessing a .38. The ME should be here soon. He can confirm."

"Or not," Dino said. "Is Barrington being a pain in the ass?"

"No more than most lawyers. He did say he wasn't fucking her."

"No," Stone said. "You asked me if I fucked her today, and I said no."

"Ah!"

"But if it's any help to you, I've never fucked her."

"How long were you alone with her today?" Dino asked.

"About fifteen minutes."

"That's long enough."

Casey laughed, and Stone rolled his eyes.

"I was just leaving," Stone said, rising. "Any other questions, call my lawyer."

"Who's your lawyer?" Casey asked.

"I am." Stone pressed the button for the elevator, and it opened immediately. He gave Dino and Casey a little wave, pressed a button, and vanished.

TWELVE

Stone walked into P. J. Clarke's and found Dino, half a drink ahead of him, at the bar. The bartender helped him catch up.

"So," Dino said. "You've been abusing my detectives again?"

"Me? Abuse? I was the *abusee*. I asked you for a good lead detective, and you sent me a jerk."

"They're mostly jerks. I can't pick and choose among them. It would be against my own established policy of whoever is available gets sent."

"'Available' is a broad term: Do you mean available as soon as Casey put down his *Hustler*?"

"I don't concern myself with my detectives' tastes in literature," Dino said. "Did you tell him the truth, the whole truth, and nothing but the truth?"

"No, I just answered his questions truthfully. Whatever he forgot to ask me wasn't covered."

"Let me ask you a really important question."

"Shoot."

"Are you hungry?"

"Starved, and that's the whole truth."

"Then follow me." Dino led the way to the rear dining room, where they were warmly received by the maître d'.

"You know," Stone said, glancing at a menu, "we weren't quite so warmly received by the maître d' before you were the commissioner."

"And the maître d' was just a headwaiter," Dino said. "Everybody wins."

"What about me?"

"You didn't get arrested this afternoon, did you?"

"That's because Casey, for the life of him, couldn't come up with a probable cause."

"Casey didn't like it that nobody saw you leave."

"Casey can go fuck himself."

"I thought that's what you were doing with the late Mrs. Charles. Did you know that people referred to her, earlier in her career, as 'Apple Annie'?"

"Yes, but I don't know why."

"Because everybody had a bite of her."

"And delicious it must have been," Stone said. "She still looked terrific at sixty, and she was still eager."

"I thought she was, maybe, forty. And how do you know she was still eager?"

"Because she had my zipper down in a flash, and I had to cite the legal ethics code to get out of there before she could do whatever it was she was going to do to me."

"How did you manage to get out?"

"I rezipped and fled the premises with a cheerful, over-the-shoulder wave. It was the last I saw of her."

"It was the last *anybody* saw of her."

"Don't point that thing at me. If I could get out of there unseen, then somebody could have gotten *in* there unseen."

"A fair point for a shyster lawyer but not for a homicide detective."

"Casey wouldn't know a fair point if it reared up and bit him on the ass." Stone snorted. "And who are you calling a shyster?"

Dino looked around. "Who else is here?"

"There are half a dozen lawyers in the room. Which of them are you impugning?"

"I could throw a dart blindfolded and hit one."

"Let's order before I use a steak knife on you," Stone said. He waved down a waiter and ordered another round and two steaks.

Dino sliced and bit into his, talking around it. "Okay, who inherits? Junior?"

"Nope. Annetta had carved him out of her will. And neither of them had any other kids."

"Who, then? The ASPCA?"

"They didn't even own a dog or a cat."

"So, who's going to get Ed Charles's ill-gotten gains?"

"My secretary."

"Joan? How did she manage that?"

"Annetta was Joan's mother's younger sister: her aunt."

"How much?"

"Just between you, me, and the bar association, north of a hundred million. A lot more if we can find it."

"Holy shit!"

"That's approximately what Joan is going to say. She typed up the will, but I withheld that part from her and typed it myself."

"Why'd you do that?"

"Because I didn't want her mooning about, dreaming of how, someday, she would be a rich woman. It would have interfered with her work, and, anyway, who knew it was going to be so soon?"

"What did you mean there's more, if you can find it?"

"Let's just say that Ed Charles's relationship with the Internal Revenue Service was, well, distant. Oh, I'm sure he has an upright accounting firm that, each year, produces a plausible tax return. But there are rumors of an offshore bank account and, locally, an oversized safety-deposit box, crammed with cash."

"And where did all this cash come from? Was he stealing from his investors?"

"I don't think Ed had any investors that he didn't invent out of thin air. A private investment company makes a wonderful money laundry, wouldn't you think?"

"I would think," Dino replied.

"I hear that Ed was banking three bookies and taking his vigorish in cash."

"What are you going to do when the Feds come sniffing around?"

"Absolutely nothing. I don't have anything to give them. They'll have heard the rumors I've heard, but I'm not in a position to substantiate them. After all, I've only been his estate's attorney for less than a week, and Annetta is no longer in a position to confide in me. The Feds will turn up with a search warrant right quick, and I'm not going to get in their way. My guess is that Ed was clever enough to conceal his assets, but he didn't do it on my watch or on my advice. I'm clean, and I'm going to remain clean. It's the Woodman & Weld way."

"And what are you going to do, if you find some of Ed's money?"

"What money?" Stone asked. "I don't know anything about any money."

THIRTEEN

When Stone got downstairs to his office the following morning, he had to make his own coffee because Joan was nowhere to be found. He checked his watch: she was always on time. "What the hell?"

The phone rang, and since Joan was not there to screen the calls, curiosity required him to answer it. "Stone Barrington."

"Hey, Stone, it's Eddie Jr."

"Why are you calling me, Junior?" Stone asked. "You're not supposed to."

"Well, this is a special occasion," Junior said, "and don't call me Junior."

"What do you want?"

"I just woke up and turned on the TV, and it said that my stepmother is dead."

"I can confirm that bit of news. Where are you, Eddie?"

"In East Hampton. I've been here for two days."

"And you just heard about Annetta?"

"I haven't been watching TV, and Annetta doesn't get the papers delivered out here. I didn't kill her. Did you kill her?"

"Certainly not," Stone replied. "Funny you should ask. The police want to ask you that same question."

"Me? I'm in the Hamptons. How could I kill her?"

"Well, there are some holes in your alibi, Eddie."

"What holes?"

"First of all, you said 'I didn't kill her,'" Stone said. "That's not an alibi, that's a contention."

"Okay, number two: I'm in East Hampton."

"Prove it."

"How do I do that?"

"Is anyone with you?"

"No, I'm alone."

"Has anybody seen you there? A maid, maybe?"

"No."

"Well, you'd better get to work thinking of some way to prove you weren't in New York, in her house yesterday afternoon."

"I told you, I was in East Hampton. I still am."

"Be sure and mention that to your lawyer, when he comes to bail you out."

"You seem to think I'm going to be arrested," Eddie said plaintively.

"I'd say you're the prime suspect unless you can come up with a plausible alibi."

"You're my lawyer, Stone. You think of a way I can do that."

"For the umpteenth time, Eddie, I am *not* your lawyer. I'm your stepmother's lawyer."

"Can't I inherit you from her?"

"That was not mentioned in her will," Stone replied.

"Speaking of her will, I get the money now, right?"

"Wrong, Eddie. She specifically excluded you as an heir."

"She can't do that after she's dead, can she?"

"She did it when she was alive and kicking," Stone replied. "You'd better get yourself a lawyer, get back to the city, and convince the police you had nothing to do with her death."

"How do I do that?"

"I thought I just explained it. First, you have to be innocent. Second, you'd better have an alibi to back up your claim of being in East Hampton. Maybe you'd better write that down. Goodbye, Eddie, and good luck staying out of prison for the rest of your life." Stone hung up. The phone began to ring again, but this time Joan answered it. She must have arrived. His intercom buzzed. "Yes?"

"Eddie Jr. on one for you. What shall I tell him?"

"As W. C. Fields once memorably said, 'Tell him to go fuck himself.' I'm sorry I don't do a better W. C. Fields impression."

"Who's W. C. Fields?"

"You're old enough to know. Eddie is going to ask you how to get himself a lawyer."

"Who should I recommend?"

"First of all, don't recommend Herbie Fisher. He'd never forgive either of us—and he might actually get Eddie off. And if he does, the phone will never stop ringing."

"Got it, I think. Any lawyer you really hate?"

"Not enough to sic Eddie Jr. on him." He thought for a moment. "Tiffany Baldwin."

"She's the federal DA for the Southern District, isn't she?"

"I heard she either retired or got booted. Anyway, she and Eddie Jr. deserve each other."

"Okay, I'll give Eddie her number."

"After that, come in and let's talk."

Ten minutes passed before Joan appeared.

"Have a seat," Stone said.

"What did I do wrong?" she asked, alarmed.

"You haven't done anything wrong," Stone said. "I just think you need to sit down to hear this."

Joan perched nervously on the edge of a chair. "What?"

"You know that Annetta is dead, right? Murdered?"

"Yes, I was here when you heard, but you know I didn't do it."

"I know that, and nobody suspects you of it."

"You mean I can get away with it?"

"What?"

"Sorry, just kidding. What else?"

"First, some questions. Did Annetta have any relatives? Brothers, sisters, cousins, distant cousins?"

"Nary a one. She's alone in the world."

"Except for you."

Joan thought about that.

"Your mother is deceased, right?"

"Right."

"Then you are Annetta's only heir."

"Well, she did leave me one hundred thousand dollars in her will."

"That was the old will. She made a new one, and she left everything to you."

"I typed her will. That wasn't in it."

"No, I typed it into her new will, so that you wouldn't know you were her only heir."

Joan blinked. "When had you planned to tell me?"

"Right after she died."

"Then why didn't you tell me immediately?"

"You're hearing about it first thing the next morning. Right now." Stone handed her his copy of the will. "Page two, near the top."

Joan read the page. "Is this legal?" she asked. "I mean, if I typed the will I could just have put my name in there, couldn't I?"

"No, I typed that page, and I can tell you, Annetta read it very carefully before signing it. This is authentic, real, witnessed, and legal. You now possess everything Annetta possessed, and that includes everything Eddie Sr. possessed."

"How much is that?"

"Remains to be seen—at least a couple hundred million dollars."

Joan collapsed onto the floor.

FOURTEEN

Stone poured a glass of water from the vessel on his desk and flicked a few drops onto Joan's face.

Joan blinked, then looked around. "Why am I on the floor?"

"You fainted."

"I never faint."

"Let's try it again. You are your aunt Annetta's sole heir, and she left you everything."

"I'm feeling faint."

Stone hoisted her into a chair. "Take a few deep breaths."

Joan did that.

"How are you feeling?"

"Better. Rich, you might say."

"That's because you're rich."

"I'm trying to get used to the idea."

"Pretty soon, you're going to want to start buying things."

"Why would I do that?"

"Because that's what people do when they become suddenly rich: they buy all the things they couldn't afford before they were rich."

Joan contemplated that. "Can I have the morning off to go shopping?"

"Take a week," Stone replied. "Get it out of your system."

"I can't take a week off," she said.

"Why not?"

"Because you can't get along without me for a week."

"You have a point," Stone said. "But I'm willing to give it a try, so you can get being rich out of your system."

"I can go shopping this weekend," she said.

"Oh, all right, if you insist."

The phone rang. "I mean," Joan said, "who would keep you from having to talk to Eddie Jr."

"The police, maybe. He's the prime suspect."

"I suppose so. Does he have an alibi?"

"He thinks he does, but he doesn't."

"What's his alibi?"

"That he's been in East Hampton for two days."

"That sounds pretty good to me," Joan said.

"Sure it does, but he can't prove it."

"Annetta has a beautiful house in East Hampton."

"No, *you* have a beautiful house in East Hampton."

"I suppose I do, don't I? Well, that's one thing I won't have to buy. Is Eddie out there?"

"He says he's been there for two days, but nobody has seen him there."

"Not good, huh?"

"Not good. Joan, will you tell me something about Eddie?"

"Sure."

"He's supposed to be so smart—Yale, law school, the bar exam. If he's that smart, why is he so unalterably stupid?"

"That's always puzzled me, too."

"He thinks he can say he was in East Hampton, and *presto!* He's in East Hampton. Is he that stupid?"

"I believe him to be," Joan said.

"And he keeps saying that I'm his lawyer when I've told him repeatedly that I'm not."

"That's Eddie Jr. for you." The phone rang.

"No, *that's* Eddie Jr.," Stone said.

Joan picked up the phone. "The Barrington Practice. Yes, he's here." She held out the phone for Stone. "It's Dino."

Stone took the phone. "Good morning."

"Not for Eddie Jr.," Dino said. "My homicide people want to talk to him. He's not at the Yale Club and not at the former Apple Annie's house."

"He says he's at her house in East Hampton, been there for two days."

"Do you believe that?" Dino asked.

"I'm withholding judgment until he can produce a witness who can put him there for that long."

"That's pretty much my policy, too. Well, I guess there's a cop or two on the homicide squad who wouldn't mind the drive out there."

"Why don't you just call that cop out there—what's-his-name? Get him to do a drive-by and ring the bell. Hang on, I'll get the address." He covered the phone. "Joan, what's the address of Annetta's—pardon me, *your* house—in East Hampton?"

"It's 69 Further Lane," Joan replied.

"Dino, it's 69 Further Lane."

"I guess I could do that. I've got his card somewhere, and he could do that."

"Proving that someone isn't where he says he is isn't so hard," Stone said. "He can handle it."

"I'll do that. Dinner tonight?"

"Patroon at seven?"

"Done." Dino hung up.

So did Stone. "Dino's going to get an East Hampton cop to drive by and prove Eddie Jr. isn't there."

"Good idea."

"I've got another one. Does Eddie have a cell phone, and if so, do you have the number?"

Joan recited the number.

Stone called Dino back and gave him the number. "Why don't you run a trace on the cell phone?"

"Couldn't hurt," Dino said. "See ya." He hung up.

"There," Stone said to Joan. "It's good to have that off my mind."

"Do you really think Eddie could have killed Aunt Annetta?" Joan asked.

"Why not?" Stone replied. "He's stupid enough."

The phone rang again, and Joan answered. "Dino, for you."

"Yeah?" Stone asked.

"I ran the trace on his cell phone."

"Where is he?"

"Apparently, he's sitting in a car outside your house."

Stone blinked. "Well, send somebody over here to arrest him."

"We'll question him at your house. If he's got an alibi, it'll save us a trip downtown."

"Whatever you like, but you have to promise me something."

"What's that?"

"If your people are going to bring him into my house, they'd better get him out when they're done."

"Agreed."

FIFTEEN

Stone sat at the table in his conference room with two detectives and stared at Edwin Charles Jr.

"Are you represented by Stone Barrington?" Detective Casey asked him.

"Yes, I am," Eddie replied.

"No, he is not represented by me," Stone said.

"Stone, just for the purpose of this interrogation, will you represent him?"

"Oh, all right. You can't ask him any questions if I don't. After this chat he'll have to find another attorney."

"Good," Casey said, turning his attention to Eddie Jr. "Now . . ."

"Eddie," Stone said.

The young man's head swiveled Stone's way. "Yes, Stone?"

"Don't answer that question, or any other question the

police ask you, until we can get an attorney who will accept your case."

Eddie turned back to face Casey. "Okay, what do you want to know?"

Casey pressed a button on a recorder. "Where have you been for the past three days?" he asked.

"Don't answer that, Eddie," Stone said.

"At my house in East Hampton."

"He doesn't have a house in East Hampton," Stone said.

"Are you trying to convict him for us?" Casey asked.

"No, I want nothing to do with him."

"You said you'd represent him for the purpose of this interrogation."

"Yes, well, I did my duty by telling him not to answer anything, as any good lawyer would do. My mistake was in thinking that he would do as I told him."

"If he wants to answer, I'm not going to stop him."

"Eddie, you don't have a house in East Hampton," Stone said. "Your stepmother cut you out of her will, so everything she has goes to Joan Robertson. It's Joan's house now."

"Nevertheless," Eddie said, "that's where I was. At 69 Further Lane."

"Was anyone there with you?" Casey asked.

"Yes, a girl named Flamingo Flame."

"That's her stripper name," Stone said. "What did her mother name her?"

"I never knew her mother," Eddie replied. "Anyway, her mother wasn't there."

"Okay," Stone said to Casey. "Ask the son of a bitch anything you like, over my protest. I'll get everything thrown out of court because he isn't represented by an attorney."

"Oh, no, you don't," Casey said. "I have you on tape saying you're representing him for the purpose of this interrogation."

"You tell the judge your story, and I'll tell him mine," Stone said. "Now, I want all of you out of my house, including Eddie. *Especially* Eddie. And since he won't answer your questions, you don't have probable cause to arrest him. Beat it, Casey."

"He was answering my questions until just a minute ago."

"He's changed his mind," Stone said. He pressed a button in front of him.

"Yes, sir?" Joan answered.

"Get your step-cousin out of here and into his car at the curb."

Joan came in, took Eddie by the wrist and elbow, and frog-marched him out of the room.

"Okay, Casey," Stone said, "we're back to where we started." He took the cassette out of Casey's recorder and put it in his jacket pocket. "Anything he said to you I will protest to a judge."

Joan came back into the conference room "Okay, Eddie is back in his car."

Stone took the cassette out of his pocket and handed it to her. "Burn this," he said. "You," he said, pointing at Casey, "you and yours: out! Joan, when you're done, make a dozen copies of Annetta's death certificate and our client agreement to represent her."

"Yes, sir." She left the room.

"Why is she still taking orders from you?" Casey asked. "She's now your client."

"I'm advising her," Stone said. "Why are you still here?"

Casey got up, beckoned to his partner, and trudged out of the building.

Joan came back. "What now?"

"Do you have a key to Annetta's former abode?"

"Yes."

"How about the East Hampton house?"

"Yes."

"Good. Now call Bob Cantor and tell him I want him to go to the apartment and change all the locks to those Israeli things he likes so much. We'll meet him there, and when he's done with that he can go out to East Hampton and change all the locks there, too."

"And why are we doing this?" she asked.

"To keep Eddie Jr. out. Tell Fred to bring out the car, and don't tell Eddie where we're going."

"Okay." Joan left the room.

Stone walked around the offices to be sure all the cops were gone, then he looked out the window into the street and saw that Eddie's car was gone, too.

Excellent!

SIXTEEN

Stone got into the Bentley with Joan and told Fred to proceed. "Do you have a remote control for the garage?" he asked Joan.

Joan took a small box from her purse and rummaged in it. "Yes," she said.

"Fred, when we get there, drive into the garage. Joan will open it for you."

"Yes, sir," Fred replied.

Shortly, they turned into the short drive, and Joan opened the garage door.

"What else is on this level?" Stone asked.

"Staff rooms and what Aunt Annetta deigned to call the 'servants' hall.'"

"Let's go there," Stone said.

They got out of the car, which was parked next to a Mercedes station wagon and two Bentleys. Stone followed Joan into a room that had probably been suggested by *Downton Abbey*. Two maids and Geoffrey, the butler, were drinking coffee and watching a soccer match on a large TV.

"Listen up," Stone said, "and mute the TV."

Everybody jumped at his command.

"This," Stone said, removing a sheet of paper from his briefcase, "is the death certificate of Annetta Charles." He set it on the table and produced another sheet. "This is a page from Mrs. Charles's will, bequeathing her entire estate to her niece, Joan Robertson, who stands beside me. This document specifically excludes Edwin Charles Jr. from inheriting any part of these estates. It also names me as the executor of her estate." He found another sheet of paper. "This," he said, "is a copy of the standard client agreement, appointing my law firm, under my supervision, to represent her, her estate, and the estate of her late husband, Edwin Charles. Is there a bulletin board in this room?"

"Yes, sir," Geoffrey replied.

"Good. Please post these documents on that board, so that all the staff may read them. And get me a list of the staff members. Does anyone not understand that Joan Robertson now owns everything that previously was owned by Edwin and Annetta Charles?"

No one spoke.

"Good. Now, your first instruction from me is that, according to Mrs. Charles's will, her stepson, Edwin Charles Jr., is barred from entering this house or any other dwelling or building owned by the Charleses. If he attempts to enter any of these buildings, you may eject him, or call the police and report him as a trespasser. Is that perfectly clear?"

Everyone nodded.

Bob Cantor entered the room, pushing a handcart containing a number of cardboard boxes.

"Good afternoon, Bob. Ladies and gentlemen, this is Mr. Robert Cantor, who will be replacing all the locks in the house with much better locks. Keys will be issued to authorized personnel by Ms. Robertson or me. Please help him in any way you can. Get started, Bob, and take a look at the security system and let me know if you consider any part of it to be inadequate."

Stone turned to Joan. "Are you familiar with this house?"

"Yes, I am. I spent time here as a child and poked my nose into every nook and cranny."

"Then let's take a look into the nooks and crannies. Lead the way."

Joan led him to an elevator and gave him a tour of the reception rooms on the lower floors, then the bedrooms on the middle floors, then finally, to the eighth floor, which contained a living room, a library, two bars, and two studies, one for each of the Charleses.

"Let's start with Ed Sr.'s study and ransack the place, every cupboard and drawer."

"What are we looking for?"

"Anything of interest, particularly keys, safe combinations, and documents dealing with banks, at home or abroad, particularly abroad."

Joan found a pair of shopping bags from Bloomingdale's and set them out, ready for use.

They had been ransacking for a few minutes when Joan held up something. "Aha!" she said.

"Aha, what?"

"Keys."

"Look for a safety-deposit box key," Stone said, then watched as she sifted through them. "We have four safety-deposit box keys," she said, holding them up.

"From what banks?"

"One from United States Trust, around the corner, two from Troutman Trust, on Madison Avenue, and one from a bank in someplace called Georgetown."

"Cayman Islands," Stone said. "Keep them all and resume ransacking."

"I'm tired," Joan said.

"There's a bar in the library," Stone said. "Let's ransack that."

"Allow me," Joan said, "as you are my guest." She found some heavy Baccarat whiskey glasses and some ice and poured two stiff Knob Creeks, handing one to Stone, then collapsing into a wing chair by the fireplace.

"Are you feeling quite at home?" Stone asked.

"Oddly, yes. I think I'll sleep here tonight."

"The master bedroom looked comfortable."

"Not until I've ransacked it, kept what I like, which will be mostly jewelry and furs, and sent the rest to Goodwill, which will blow their minds."

"Good thinking. Now, I think we should discuss your successor."

"My successor? Are you firing me?"

"Surely a person of your great wealth and standing in the community would not wish to continue working for me."

"Why not? It's the most fun I've ever had. You can refer to me as your assistant, though, and not your secretary. I'll want to hire my own secretary."

"Would you like a raise?"

"Just for form's sake, you can double my present salary."

"Done. And hire whoever you like and pay her or him whatever you see fit."

"Tomorrow," she said, "after we've ransacked the safety-deposit boxes."

SEVENTEEN

Stone met Joan at United States Trust on the Upper East Side just as the doors opened. He noted that Joan was pushing a large, wheeled suitcase. He had dealt before with the manager, a Mr. Hedger, and they were shown into his office.

"Good morning, Stone," Hedger said. "Please have a seat."

"I have brought you new business," Stone said, and introduced Joan. "Ms. Robertson is the niece and only survivor of Annetta Charles, and thus her heir."

"My condolences and my congratulations," Hedger said to her.

Stone opened his briefcase and handed Hedger some documents. "This is Mrs. Charles's death certificate, along with that of her husband, Edwin Sr., who predeceased her. Also, a copy of her last will and testament, which makes Joan her only heir. Please note that Edwin Charles Jr. is explicitly excluded from any inheritance and that a trust has been provided to meet his basic needs. Don't let Junior tell you any different."

"I understand," Hedger said. "We will be closing his accounts. It will be a relief not to have Junior as a customer any longer."

Stone handed Hedger a safety-deposit box key. "We assume that this is the key issued to Ed Sr. when he opened his account."

Hedger checked the number on his computer. "Confirmed," he said.

"Please change the ownership to Ms. Robertson. Also, any other accounts opened by Ed Sr. or Annetta."

Hedger did some more computer work, then took a card from a desk drawer. "Ms. Robertson, may I have your address and phone numbers, and a sample of your signature?"

Joan completed the card. "I'd like Mr. Barrington to be a cosigner on all my accounts," she said, "but not a co-owner." She smirked a little at Stone.

Hedger handed Stone the card.

"There," Stone said, signing it with a flourish. "That will be sufficient for me to steal her blind."

"Just try it," Joan said.

Hedger gave her a book showing checkbook styles, and she chose one.

"We'll messenger you your checks tomorrow," Hedger said. He consulted his computer again, then scribbled something on a card and handed it to her. "This is the current balance of your checking account and your household account, from which Mrs. Charles paid her staff and other expenses."

Joan glanced at the card and tucked it into her purse.

"How else can I help you?" Hedger asked.

"I'd like to visit my safety-deposit box," she replied.

"Please follow me." Hedger led them to an elevator, which went two floors down. They emerged into a vault containing many boxes, and he introduced Joan to the guard in charge. "Ms. Robertson would like to visit her box," Hedger said to the guard. "Ms. Robertson, I'll leave you in his capable hands. Feel free to call me whenever I may be of help."

The guard went to unlock the box, using the bank's key and Joan's.

"What is the balance of the personal checking account?" Stone asked.

"Two hundred and eighty-eight thousand and change," she replied. "And half again as much in the household account." The guard escorted them to a private room, where he unlocked a large box and returned the key to her. "Please let me know when you're ready to leave, Ms. Robertson, and I'll secure the box."

"Thank you," Joan said. "Stone, you open it."

"Why are you looking so worried?" he asked, opening the box.

"I'm afraid it might be empty." She peered into the box. "How much do you think that is?" she asked, pointing.

Stone looked into the box and found it nearly filled with bundles of hundred-dollar bills. "I should think something between a million and a half and two million dollars."

"Oh, dear," she said, leaning against the box for support.

Stone said, "I hope you're not going to faint again."

"Not this time." She hoisted her suitcase onto the table and opened it. "Let's see if this will hold a million dollars," she said, and the two of them started transferring bundles while keeping a running tab. They stopped at one million, and the suitcase was only half full.

"Let's leave the rest here for a rainy day," Joan said.

They left the bank, and Fred put the case into the trunk.

"Let's go see what Troutman Trust has in store for us."

Fred drove them to the bank and took the case out of the trunk. They met the local manager, then repeated their earlier performance and were taken downstairs to the vault, where two steel boxes, both larger than those at U.S. Trust, awaited them.

Stone surveyed the contents of the two boxes. "I'd say something in the region of five million."

They filled Joan's suitcase from one of the boxes, then had them locked away.

"Let's go home," Joan said.

"Your house or mine?" Stone asked.

"Yours. You've got some empty space in your various safes."

They went back to Stone's house, where Joan opened the big Excelsior safe, and they got two million dollars stuffed inside.

"I'll stow the remainder at my new house," she said. "After work."

She went back to her desk and started doing what she did every day.

"We'll need to have a talk about taxes," Stone said.

"Taxes? What taxes?"

"I'll need to take a look at Ed Sr's. final tax return," Stone said. "Then you can decide how much time you're willing to do."

EIGHTEEN

At mid-morning the next day Joan came into Stone's office. "Yes, sir?"

Stone tapped on a stack of files on his desk. "I've been through all this, and it appears that Ed Sr. had declared all the cash in the U.S. Trust box as income and paid taxes on it. The estate, of course, pays any further taxes due to the IRS and the state, and everything else is yours, free of taxes."

"How much, net to me?"

"The investment accounts are, as you might imagine, fat. And together they contain about three hundred million dollars, after any taxes. My best guess is $375,000,000, not including the cash in the Troutman Trust boxes, which has not, so far, been reported. Let's call that another five million."

"So, I'm worth $380,000,000?"

"Considerably more than that. We haven't talked about the

real estate and other property. Add another $100,000,000 for that, so well over $450,000,000."

"Whew!" Joan said.

"Now, let's talk about greed."

"'Greed'?"

"How greedy are you?"

"So-so greedy, I guess."

"There's a way to get the Troutman cash out of the country and into an offshore bank account, too. But there's a risk," Stone said.

"Tell me about it."

"I fly you down to the Bahamas, and we check into a nice hotel for a few days. The next day, you charter a light airplane, under an assumed name, and you fly to Georgetown, in the Cayman Islands, south of Jamaica, no more than an hour's flight. You take your luggage off the charter and to a bank in the city—there are many to choose from. You open a numbered account—no name on it—and deposit your cash there. Then you fly back to the Bahamas, lie on the beach for a few days, then fly home. The bank will issue you a credit card that works anywhere in the world, drawing on your Cayman cash."

"What's the risk?"

"You have to fill out a form before you leave the States declaring any funds or financial instruments that amount to more than ten thousand dollars. Lying on that form is a felony, with a big fine, forfeiture of your cash, and, maybe, jail time. But U.S. Customs may neglect to inspect your luggage."

"And the alternative?"

"Declare the cash to the IRS now, pay the taxes, and live happily ever after."

"I like that one," she said. "I'm rich enough without cheating the IRS."

"So you won't be vacationing in the Bahamas?"

"Maybe next year, sans cash."

"I am greatly relieved," Stone said.

"I'm going to spend the weekend at my new house, going through Aunt Annetta's things and deciding what to keep."

"You might look around the house and see if there are any pictures or sculptures that you can't stomach, and put together a list for auction. Same with jewelry."

"Good idea."

"I must say, your aunt Annetta had very good taste in furnishings and décor."

"She had dreadful taste in those things," Joan said. "Ralph Lauren has good taste. His people did the whole place."

"That would explain it."

"By the way, I've hired a secretary."

"Who is she?"

"Her name is Alberta Page," Joan said.

"Al for short?"

"Peaches."

"What?"

"Alberta is a species of peach."

"Peaches Page. I like it."

"She starts tomorrow, but neither of us will be in; we'll be working on the house together."

"Can I help?" Stone asked.

"You'd just be in the way."

"Right."

"See you Monday."

"Hold on. I'm going out in a few minutes," Stone said, "got an appointment downtown, so turn on the answering machine."

"Okay."

Stone got out of the Bentley in Little Italy, a short distance from the La Boheme coffeehouse. He made a call. "I'm outside," he said.

"Back room" was the reply. The man hung up.

Stone walked into the coffee shop, and a waiter caught his eye and nodded toward a door at the rear of the room.

Stone knocked, then entered. A man in his mid-thirties sat alone at a table and waved him to a seat. "Vito Datilla," he said, offering his hand.

"Stone Barrington." He sat down. The young man, he knew, was referred to locally as Datilla the Hun, as was his father before him.

"What can I do for you?"

"I represent the estates of Edwin and Annetta Charles," Stone said.

The Hun's eyebrows went up. "I see."

"Perhaps not."

"You do not wish to continue our business relationship?" He sounded hurt.

"The Charleses' heir does not wish to. No offense intended."

"I'll try not to take any."

"I would be grateful to you."

"So, you're the big-time, uptown lawyer?"

"I have dealings in all sorts of places."

"Some friends of mine told me about you. They were impressed, so I'm impressed."

"That's kind of you."

"So, let me guess: The heir wants Ed's money back?"

"That puts it succinctly."

"Now, why would I want to give a refund?"

"It's the heir's decision. It's her money."

"We've been doing very well, lending that money."

"I expect so. All the more reason for a refund to be painless."

"Shelling out three million clams is never painless."

"It is, if they're not your clams."

"Suppose I make your heir an offer?"

"Anything in excess of three million clams would be welcome."

Datilla laughed. "I hear you got another friend, who's the police commissioner."

"I would never mention his name in a transaction such as this."

"Still, if I decline to refund, he might take offense on your behalf."

"He will never hear of it."

"If I refund?"

"He wouldn't hear of it from me, even if you decline to do the right thing."

"So, you're not threatening me?"

"That would be disrespectful," Stone said. "I have every respect for you. I hope you will respect my client, as well."

"You realize, Barrington, that there's no paper on all this. Why would I refund money I don't have to?"

"Nothing requires you to . . . except honor."

Datilla blinked. "I'll give you this, Barrington: you know how to handle a ticklish situation."

"I hope so. I do that for a living."

"Would you like to represent me sometime? I can always use a legit lawyer."

"I would prefer to keep our relationship as it is. I hope you understand."

"Explain it to me."

"I have partners. We all have clients who have certain expectations of us regarding our other clients. We have to respect their wishes in that regard."

"Delicately put."

"Thank you."

Datilla reached under the table for something. Stone tensed, half expecting him to come up with a shotgun. Instead, he placed a battered suitcase on the table. "There you are," he said. "Would you like to count it?"

Stone shook his head. "I trust you," he said. "And, anyway,

the bank will count it later. If there's a discrepancy, I'll send you either a bill or a refund."

Datilla laughed again and made a shooing motion with his hands.

"I'm a busy man," he said. "Get outta here." He offered his hand.

Stone shook it and got out of there.

NINETEEN

Stone sat Joan down and put a document before her. "This is Ed Sr.'s estate tax return. If you read it carefully, you may note an additional declaration of three million dollars in income, which we have not previously discussed."

"Then why are we discussing it now?" Joan asked.

"It's like this: Ed Sr. had a financial relationship with Dominic Datilla, affectionately known to some as Datilla the Hun."

"What kind of financial relationship?"

"Ed loaned Datilla money," Stone replied.

"He loaned the Mafia money?"

"He did, and at a great profit to himself. Datilla distributed the money to his capos and their loan sharks loaned it, in varying amounts, to gamblers and as loans to those who could not obtain credit at banks. All at a very high interest rate. In return, Ed Sr. received a large payment in cash weekly. Some of it is the money in the Excelsior safe."

"Ah."

"I have given Ed's accountant the three million dollars he loaned Datilla, in cash, which was reported on Ed's tax return as income, so you're all square with the IRS."

"Datilla returned Ed's money?"

"By the way, we are running out of safe space to store your millions. Ed may have a large safe somewhere in the house that you can store it in, and the combination will probably be concealed nearby."

"Or in Ed's notebook," she said, "which I found in his desk drawer."

"If he doesn't have such a safe, I suggest that you measure an available space in the house, then drop into Empire Safes—on East Thirty-Ninth Street—and order a new one to fill the empty space."

"What a good idea!" she said. "I must say, I'm impressed that you persuaded Datilla to return the principal. How did you do that?"

Stone shrugged. "I put it to him as a matter of honor. Those gentlemen take honor very seriously. And on occasion, they choose to live by it."

"And Datilla did?"

"He did. I was very relieved because his honor was all we had going for us. He could have booted me out into the street, but he didn't. We could hardly sue him."

"I should write him a thank-you note."

Stone laughed. "That might amuse him, but let's let sleeping mafiosi lie."

"As you wish. Where do I sign the return?"

"Your accountant has already signed it."

"Oh, good. Now all I have to do is to put all the household accounts in my name, and I'm done."

"May I make a suggestion?"

"Of course."

"Give your household staff a ten percent raise. It will stand you in good stead with them."

"What a good idea!"

"I'm glad you think so."

The phone rang. Joan answered the one on Stone's desk, then handed it to him. "Dino."

"Good morning, Commissioner."

"Yeah, sure. You know where I can put my hands on Eddie Jr.?"

"He was parked outside my house last time I knew that, so you had a shot."

"That didn't work out."

"He's living at the Yale Club, I think."

"Well, he's got some stuff there, but no sign of his corpus. Does he have another address?"

"I don't think so. Annetta's will barred him from her customary lairs. And we've changed the locks on all of those. Do you have a charge?"

"I'm thinking murder one," Dino said.

"You finally think he killed Annetta?"

"Who else would profit from her death?"

"Well, Joan would and did. But she's hardly a suspect."

"We've already removed her name from the list."

"Eddie won't profit from Annetta's death, either. She left him a generous bequest in a trust, but cut him off from everything else."

"Did Eddie know that at the time?"

"I don't know. She may have told him. Or she may have just let him find out about it later, when she wouldn't be present for the resulting tantrum."

"Okay, then. He can try proving at his trial that he didn't know he was disinherited."

"He can certainly try."

"Can he bring a civil suit about the will?"

"Sure, but he won't win. She had no obligation to tell him that she had cut him off at the knees."

"Then we can make a case that he thought he was inheriting everything."

"Why not? Given the life he's led, he must have done *something* that he should do time for."

"Has he got any hangouts where we might find him?"

"Well, he used to hang out at P. J. Clarke's now and again, but after his last visit there, he won't be welcome anymore. Of course, that may not stop him from trying to get a table. The guy is brazen."

"That will make it all the more fun when we catch up to him."

"Have you put out an APB?"

"Nah, if we do that, he'll hear about it and go to ground or leave town. Did Annetta have any other houses anywhere?"

"The place in East Hampton. I'll ask Joan about others."

"Dinner tonight? Rotisserie Georgette?"

"See you at seven."

TWENTY

At Georgette's, Stone was greeted by the strains of a jazz group at the end of the bar, inside the front door. He liked that. Dino was waving from a table near the other end of the bar.

Stone fell into his chair.

"They don't sell Knob Creek here," Dino said. "I ordered you a High Rock." This was a New York State bourbon from a private distillery near the Connecticut border.

"That will do me," Stone said. "Any luck locating our Black Dog?"

"Is that what you call Eddie Jr.?"

"It's what his stepmother called him. She said he was too awful to be a black sheep. What's your evidence against Junior?" Stone asked.

"Three things: One, he has a motive. Two, he lied about his whereabouts. And three, we can't find him."

"The first two should be helpful in court, but not necessarily so. I think a judge would find your third reason to be your own fault."

"Sometimes it's hard to find people who don't want you to find them."

"Sad for cops, isn't it? You think all suspects should just present themselves at the nearest police station and ask to be locked up?"

"I think there oughta be a law to that effect," Dino said.

Stone's phone rang. "Yes?"

"It's Joan. Something just occurred to me about Ed Jr."

"What's that?"

"He likes jazz."

"Jazz . . . huh. Thanks, I'll keep that in mind."

"I've got the master suite ready to move into. I'm just waiting for Aunt Annetta's unwanted stuff to dematerialize."

"You want to join Dino and me for dinner?"

"Thanks, but I've already ordered Chinese from Evergreen."

"Enjoy using the chopsticks."

"I'll do my best." She hung up.

"That was Joan?"

"Yes, she's gradually moving into her late aunt's house."

"What's the square footage over there?"

"Ten or twelve thousand square feet, depending on if you count the garage and the servants' quarters."

"I guess people as rich as Annetta still call them servants."

"Mostly, I think, they call them staff."

"It's just you, then, who calls them servants?"

"I call them staff, too."

"Is there a ballroom?" Dino asked.

"I believe so, but I haven't waltzed across it."

"How old is the house?"

"Turn of the century—the last century."

"Then they must have stables, too."

"Maybe they relabeled them as the garage. On the other hand, they could have had cars about that time."

"What was that about jazz?" Dino asked.

"Joan says we should look in jazz clubs."

"Well," Dino said, "this is a jazz club, sort of. I mean, there's a jazz group at the other end of the bar."

"Did you see Junior up there on the way in?"

"No."

"Neither did I. That eliminates this joint from the list of jazz clubs."

A waiter appeared, and they ordered a roast duck and a bottle of good red wine. And another drink.

Georgette stopped at their table to greet them.

"Georgette," Stone said, "why don't you stock Knob Creek?"

"We sell High Rock, instead. The owners are friends."

"You couldn't sell both?"

"If I tried, people might not order my friends' bourbon."

"You have a point."

"I'll send you one on the house." She departed for other tables.

The bar area began to get very crowded with people

waiting for tables. Somebody cranked up the sound system a bit, so the jazz group could be heard better.

Stone peered through the crowd. "Funny, I thought I caught a glimpse of Eddie Jr.," he said.

"Where?"

"Down at the other end of the bar, where the jazz is coming from."

Dino followed Stone's nose. "It's pretty crowded down there."

"Want to take a stroll and see?" Stone asked.

"What for? A 'stroll' in these circumstances just means elbowing people out of the way and pissing them off. Then, if we found him, he wouldn't come quietly, and we'd cause a scene. But if he did come quietly, we'd lose the duck while we wait for a squad car to pick him up, and I'm hungry."

"Why don't you just call the Nineteenth's homicide squad and tell them there's a reported sighting of Junior here. Let them figure it out."

"That's a thought."

"Better yet, tell them to wait outside until Junior leaves, so we won't piss off Georgette by making the bust at her bar."

"An even better idea," Dino said, getting out his cell phone. He spoke for a minute or so, then hung up. "They're on it," he said. "You want you and me to back them up?"

"Not if the duck comes before then. I confess I'm more interested in the duck than in Eddie Jr. He's your problem, after all."

"No, he's the squad's problem now. I'm just as interested in the duck as you are."

"We'll see the lights when they show up."

"No, I told them not to use the lights and sirens. There'll just be an unmarked car or two."

Stone saw a car stop outside. Four burly men got out and headed for the restaurant.

"They're here," Stone said.

"So is the duck," Dino said, tucking his napkin under his chin.

TWENTY-ONE

They were halfway through the roast duck when Dino looked toward the bar and pointed his knife. "Hey, my guys got Junior!" The four cops were muscling a protesting man toward the front door. The jazz group leaned back, so as not to get knocked down.

"No, they don't have him."

"What do you mean? They're getting him cuffed."

"It sure looks like him, but trust me, that's not Junior."

"Then why are they cuffing him?"

"Go figure. They'll sort it out at the precinct."

Georgette appeared at their table. "Dino," she said. "Your cops are dragging one of my best customers out of here."

"You mean Eddie Charles Jr.?"

"No, I mean Marv Kelly, my favorite billionaire."

"Dino," Stone said, "go save the NYPD fifty million bucks."

Dino put down his utensils, wiped his greasy face with his

napkin, and leaned into the crowd, using his elbows. He reached the front door just in time to stop the cops from dragging the billionaire into the street. Stone watched and laughed as Dino flashed his badge and yelled something at the cops. He uncuffed the man, dusting off his shoulders and apologizing profusely, while shouting at the cops. He turned the man around and walked him back to his seat at the bar, then produced his card and made the "anything I can ever do for you, call me" speech. It seemed to be working. He signaled the bartender to bring a double of what the man had been drinking. Then he backed away, still apologizing, and finally made it back to the table.

"Good job," Stone said.

"It's your fault," Dino said. "You didn't tell me he was the wrong guy."

"I *did* tell you he was the wrong guy, but you were so occupied with the duck that you ignored me until Georgette intervened. You got there just in time to avoid the attention of the *Post*'s front page tomorrow morning. Chances are, you'll still make Page Six." That was the newspaper's gossip column. "If you're lucky, you'll come off as the hero who saved the day. If you're not lucky, then you'll be explaining things to the mayor first thing tomorrow morning."

Dino returned his attention to the duck, only to find that Stone had eaten all the best parts while he was attending to the matter out front. "This is what I get for being a good guy?"

"No, it's what you *don't* get."

"I was hungry!"

"I was hungrier. And I thought you were heading for the precinct."

Georgette came by the table. "Thank you, Dino, for fixing something that was your fault anyway."

Dino could only sputter.

"There's plenty of bread left," Stone said.

"I want duck!"

"They'll have to start all over. At this time of night, it'll take at least an hour. Order some cheesecake, that'll fill you up."

"Yeah, but it's not duck."

Dino grabbed a passing waiter's sleeve. "Another duck," he said.

"We're all out, Commissioner. You got the last one."

Dino slumped in his chair, finally defeated.

"How about a nice slice of cheesecake, on the house?"

"Oh, all right." It came, and he wolfed it down. "Okay," he said, "let's get out of here."

They threaded their way through the crowd at the bar. Dino paused to apologize to the billionaire again.

As Stone passed he said to the man, "They treated you very badly. I hope you're suing the NYPD."

"Good idea," the man said. "You want to be my witness?"

"I didn't have a good enough view," Stone said. "Maybe next time." By the time Stone got into the street, Dino was slamming the car door, and the vehicle drove off without him, leaving him in the gutter, shouting at the rear bumper.

It had started to rain. Stone hoofed it over to Fifth Avenue and finally got a cab, but he was soaked.

TWENTY-TWO

Stone was at his desk the following morning when Joan buzzed. "Dino, on one."

Stone picked up. "Thanks for the lift home last night."

"Thanks for the duck," Dino replied.

"No thanks necessary. I put it on your tab."

"Of course you did."

"You'll be happy to know I got soaking wet before I could find a cab."

"You're right, I feel better already."

"I suppose you called about Junior."

"Yeah, I did. Where the fuck is your client?"

"You know, I think I'll have this message printed up on cards, so I can just hand them out to people like you, instead of explaining. To wit: I DO NOT REPRESENT EDWIN CHARLES JR. IN ANY CAPACITY. I AM ONLY THE ATTORNEY TO HIS PARENTS'

ESTATE AND, AS SUCH, ACT AS HIS TRUSTEE. How's that? Plain enough?"

"I understand perfectly."

"Wonderful, I'll send you a few cards for distribution to anyone you meet who wants to know anything about the kid."

"Okay, so where is he?"

"Why do you think I know? Give me one shred of evidence of that."

"Only a shred?"

"A shred will do nicely."

"You're his fucking trustee."

"That does not meet the legal standard of 'shred.' It only means that, occasionally, he might call me and ask for more money. I say no, then I hang up. It's a brief conversation. I live in the hope that, one day soon, he will get the picture and stop calling."

"Do you ever get mail from him?"

"Well, last week he sent me his dry-cleaning bill, which was returned, marked 'Addressee unknown.' Such is the extent of our postal communication. Tell you what: I'll forward all his mail to you."

"Why don't I believe you?"

"Because you are an intensely suspicious person who cannot abide the truth, even when it rises up and bites you on the ass."

"Give me just a hint on how to find him."

"Okay, take the A train to Harlem—with apologies to Duke

Ellington—get off, have a look around the station, then take it back to Grand Central, and do the same."

"It would save us both a lot of time if you would just give me some information about Junior," Dino said.

"Okay, I'll save you a lot of time: if ever again you call me with reference to the aforementioned Black Dog, I will unceremoniously hang up on you. Use your free time well." Stone hung up to demonstrate his intention. He buzzed Joan.

"Yes, sir?"

"From now on, should Dino phone me, question him on his reason for calling. If any reference is made to Eddie Jr., hang up on him."

"What if he calls back?"

"Same drill."

"Whatever you say, boss."

"Hey, how did your housecleaning go?"

"Goodwill was stunned by what was delivered to them. I suggested they hold an auction. The feather boas alone will bring in thousands."

"Annetta actually wore feather boas?"

"She did. Don't get me started on her thongs."

"So, are you in residence now?"

"I will be by dinnertime."

"Dinner all alone? Awww."

"Don't worry, I inherited an excellent cook, who has already been warned that if I gain so much as a pound, she will be taken out and shot."

"That should ensure you many terrible meals."

"Maybe, but I won't gain a pound."

They both hung up. A moment later, Joan buzzed again. "Dino, on one."

"Did you hang up on him?"

"I couldn't. He didn't mention what's-his-name."

Stone pressed the button. "Steady, now, don't forget and bring up Junior, or I'll have to hang up."

"Dinner tonight?"

"Didn't we have dinner last night?"

"Not quite. P. J. Clarke's at seven?"

"If you're sure you can contain your curiosity about the kid."

"I'll try." Dino hung up.

TWENTY-THREE

Stone walked into P. J. Clarke's and was shocked to find Dino at the bar chatting amiably with a beautiful woman—a stunner, with bright red hair and green eyes. "Good evening," he said, offering his hand. "I'm Stone Barrington. Who in the world are you?"

"I'm Bridget Tierney," she replied, shaking his hand.

"I hope my friend, Mr. Peabody, here, hasn't been bothering you."

"'Peabody'? He told me his name was Dino Bacchetti."

"I'm very much afraid that he tells people that all the time, especially attractive women. He also tells a preposterous story about being the New York City police commissioner. Did he try that on you?"

"I'm afraid so," she said, searing Dino with a glance.

"I'm glad I came along before any real harm was done. Did he invite you to dinner?"

"He did."

"I'm afraid he can't afford to dine in good restaurants. He would just stick you with the check."

"Now that you mention it," she said, "he does look pretty sneaky, doesn't he?"

"He's married, too. Did he mention that?"

"No," she replied, "he did not."

"Oh, yes, to a fine woman who has to support him and their four children. She's taken away his credit cards."

"All right," Dino said, "this has gone far enough."

"The truth hurts, doesn't it?" Stone asked. "I wonder, Bridget, if you'd like to dine with me, instead? You won't get the check, I promise."

"I think I'd like that very much," she said, hopping off her barstool.

"Right this way." Stone led her to a table, with Dino tagging along like a puppy, denying all Stone had said.

"Really, Dino, this has gone far enough, hasn't it?"

But Dino was showing Bridget his badge and ID.

"It's a very good fake, isn't it?" Stone asked Bridget. "He's been using it for years."

Dino laid down his business card, as well.

"The badge and ID look pretty real," she said.

"There's a shop in Times Square that will sell you one just like it. You, too, can be police commissioner!"

The maître d' approached. "Excuse me, Commissioner," he said, "there's a phone call for you."

"I'll be right back," Dino said.

"It's all part of the act," Stone said. "We'll see no more of him tonight."

"Thank you for rescuing me, Stone."

"It's all part of the service."

"Tell me, are you the infamous Stone Barrington I'm forever reading about on Page Six, of the *Post*?"

Stone shrugged. "They do have a way of making up things about me," he said. "Don't believe everything you read in the columns."

"Are you a partner at Woodman & Weld?"

"A senior partner. Have you heard of us?"

"I'm a partner at Woodside & Weems," she said, naming a white-shoe firm.

"Allow me to congratulate you. Have I stolen any of your clients?"

"Not even close."

"It's a relief to hear that. It's so embarrassing when competing firms accuse me."

"When is poor Dino coming back?" she asked.

"Oh, I think he's all out of gall for the evening."

Dino returned and sat down on the other side of Bridget. "Did he jump you while I was gone?"

"No," she replied, "but he was thinking about it. I could tell."

"Show her your scar from the bullet wound, Dino. That's always very convincing."

"All right," Bridget said. "This has gone far enough, both of you." The waiter approached. "I'd like a strip steak, medium, and a loaded baked potato, please," she said. "And I don't care who pays for it."

Stone and Dino ordered, too. "She's paying," Stone said to the waiter.

After dinner, Stone invited Bridget back to his house for a drink. "I'm afraid Dino will insist on coming," he said.

They drove down to Stone's house, and he let them in.

"The house really belongs to a friend of Stone's," Dino said. "He made the mistake of giving Stone a key."

"Who's the friend?" she asked.

"A terrible person named Edwin Charles Jr."

"I know Eddie. He's not so terrible. I saw him at lunch today, in fact."

"At lunch where?" Dino asked.

"The Grill," she replied. "Used to be the Four Seasons."

"There you are, Dino," Stone said. "Right under your nose the whole time."

"Who was he lunching with?"

"The managing partner of my law firm," she said.

"Whatever you do, don't hire Junior," Stone leapt in. "He tried that with us, and we barred him from the building. He tried to bribe the head of our personnel department."

"I heard that he actually had bribed the fellow, and that he got tossed out on his ear."

"You mustn't believe every rumor you hear," Stone said. "Cognac?"

"Oh, I checked out the story. It was all perfectly true. Yes, cognac, please."

"He's a suspect in the murder of his stepmother, Annetta Charles," Dino said.

"He's the *only* suspect," Stone echoed. "And Dino and his merry band of detectives can't find him anywhere."

"I heard he's living at his club," Bridget said.

"The Yale Club?" Dino asked.

"The Athletic Club," she replied.

"Excuse me for a moment, I have to make a call." Dino stepped out of the study.

"Well," Stone said, "that got rid of him, at last. Do you think you and I might have dinner without him very soon?"

"I think we might," she replied.

Dino returned, breathless. "We nailed him at the Athletic Club!" he said. "I gotta go."

"Of course you do, Dino," Stone said. "Don't let the doorknob hit you in the ass!" He turned his attention back to Bridget.

TWENTY-FOUR

Stone woke slowly. There was a pile of red hair on his shoulder, and his right arm was numb to the fingertips. A smooth leg was thrown over his own leg. A bell rang, signaling the arrival of the dumbwaiter.

Stone extracted his arm from under Bridget's head and tried to move his fingers, which didn't work. He got up and went to the dumbwaiter, slapping his right hand. Pins and needles ensued, and a moment later he could grip one side of the tray, sort of. He set it on the foot of the bed, then found a wicker stand, which he set between them. He kissed Bridget on the ear with a loud smack, and she raised her head and looked around.

"Hmm, I'm in a naked man's bedroom," she said to nobody in particular.

"It is I," Stone said. "Breakfast is ready." He found the remote control and raised the back of the bed until she was pointed at the tray.

"Ummm," she muttered.

"I'll take that as an affirmative," Stone said, arranging a starched linen napkin over her naked breasts. "Bon appétit!"

"What?"

"That's French for 'wake up and eat.'"

She picked up a sausage and bit off the end. "Oh, yes!" she enthused, grabbing her fork and digging in.

They were both quiet until the food had been consumed.

"Did you kidnap me and bring me here?" she asked.

"Au contraire!" Stone replied. "That's French for 'you couldn't be more wrong.' My last memory is of you slinging me over your shoulder and throwing me into bed, then tearing off my clothes."

"My last memory is somewhat different," she said. "You were removing mine."

"I tried to help," Stone replied. "Anyway, it was a good breakfast, wasn't it?"

"The sex wasn't awful, either."

"We do what we can."

"You do pretty good. What is the hour?"

"A quarter past seven. Time to do it again."

"That will have to wait for another occasion," she said, hopping out of bed. "I have an eight o'clock meeting, and I can't wear the dress I was wearing."

"My loss. May we schedule a rematch?"

"How's your schedule for this evening?" she asked, pulling on a thong.

"Wide open," Stone said. "Seven o'clock here? My cook will do for us."

"Where am I?"

Stone gave her the address.

"Is that Turtle Bay? With the garden?"

"It is. We'll dine in the garden, if you like."

"I like." She gathered up her clothes and ran into the bathroom.

"There's a fresh toothbrush in there!" Stone shouted.

She stuck her head outside the door, foaming at the mouth. "Found it!" she said, sort of.

She departed the bathroom with her hair newly brushed, planted a big kiss on his lips, and ran for the door. "See you at seven!" she shouted over her shoulder.

Stone switched on the TV and made do with *Morning Joe.*

His phone rang. "Yes?"

"Is this Stone Barrington?"

"Yes, you got lucky."

"This is the night court bailiff. We've got an arraignment scheduled for an Edwin Charles Jr., and he says you're representing him."

"Never heard of him," Stone replied. "Tell him to ask for a public defender."

"Really? On a murder one charge?"

"The experience will do him good." Stone hung up.

Almost immediately, the phone rang again. This time it

was Joan. "I've got Eddie Jr. on the other line," she said. "He's being arraigned on a murder one charge, and he wants you."

"I believe you have your instructions with regard to Junior," Stone said. "Didn't I charge you with finding him a lawyer?"

"Well, ah, I've been pretty busy, what with the house and all."

"Be sure and tell Junior that, when you tell him his attorney is on the way, and it is not I."

He hung up.

Eventually, shaved, showered, and dressed, Stone made his way downstairs to his office, where he found a beautiful blonde in a short dress arranging the mail on his desk.

"Hi," she said. "I'm Peaches Page."

"Of course you are." Stone remembered that Joan had hired her. "Has Joan surfaced yet?"

"She called from a cab. She had to go down to the courthouse for something."

"Probably picking out a lawyer for Eddie Jr. in the hallway outside the courtroom. That's where the best ones hang out."

"Really?"

"Not really, but murderers can't be choosy."

"I know Eddie Jr.," Peaches replied. "He couldn't be a murderer."

"I'm sorry you've had that unfortunate experience, but when you've hung around law offices long enough, you'll learn that absolutely anybody could be a murderer."

"But his mother?"

"Stepmother."

"Oh, well . . ."

"Yes."

They heard the street door slam. Joan came in, dropping a couple of stuffed shopping bags and getting out of her coat.

"How did your tour of our courts turn out?" Stone asked.

"He got somebody from the law firm Annetta fired when she hired you," she said. "Oh, the lawyer wants two million dollars from Eddie's trust for bail."

Stone thought about that.

"Well?" Joan asked.

"I'm thinking about it."

"Well, it's Eddie's money—eventually."

"Okay, but cut his allowance in half, until the trust has been reimbursed."

"I'll get it done."

"No rush. A tour of Rikers Island will be a character-building experience for Junior."

TWENTY-FIVE

Stone's front doorbell rang a little after seven. He checked the camera, then buzzed Bridget Tierney in. He received her and gave her a welcoming hug and a kiss.

"It's raining out there," she said, handing him her umbrella and raincoat. "I hope you're flexible about our dining arrangements."

"We're doing it in my study instead," he said, leading the way and seating her on the sofa before the fireplace, which was ablaze. "Drink?"

"What's the house specialty?"

"A vodka gimlet."

"I'll take a chance."

Stone went to the little freezer in the bar and poured two vodka gimlets into champagne glasses, then handed her one. "Cheers."

She sipped, then put a hand to her breast. "Oh, that's breathtaking!"

"I'm glad you think so." He sat down beside her. "How was your day?"

"Interesting. I made my first court appearance for Woodside & Weems. Nothing big. I hope we don't talk about work," she said. "It gets boring fast."

"Agreed, no work."

"And your day?"

"I've promised not to talk about work," Stone said, "and today was work."

"What shall we talk about then?" she asked.

"You choose. I'll cooperate."

"All right, give me your sixty-seconds biography."

"Okay," Stone said, taking a deep breath. "Born, Greenwich Village, P.S. Six, NYU prelaw, followed by NYU Law, took a ride with a couple of cops on duty, liked it, applied for the police academy. Fourteen years on the street, ten as a detective. Took a bullet in the knee, invalided out of the NYPD. How much time do I have left?"

"Enough, go ahead."

"Inherited this house from a great-aunt, got into debt renovating it. Then a friend at Woodman & Weld offered me a job, if I took the bar exam cram course. Then I passed the exam. Lived happily ever after, so far. Your turn."

"Born in Delano, Georgia, a small town, public schools, University of Georgia, UGA law school. Came to New York and worked as a public defender because there wasn't any other work. Got good at it. Then got an offer from Woodside & Weems a few weeks ago. I had whipped one of theirs in court, and they were impressed."

"Great," Stone said. "Now what shall we talk about?"

"I'm drawing a blank. I guess we're going to have to talk about work."

"Okay, what would you like to know?"

"What do you work on at Woodman & Weld?"

"I started with the cases the firm didn't want to be seen to be handling—you know, client's wife has a DUI, client's son accused of date rape at college, like that. Eventually, I began to make some rain, and they took me seriously. Now I'm a senior partner, handling a number of big accounts."

"Such as?"

"Strategic Services, a big security firm. Steele Insurance Group, self-explanatory. Centurion Pictures, in L.A. I serve on those three boards, as well. What has Woodside & Weems put you to work on?"

"Cases like the ones you started out with, the ones they don't want to know about. They didn't have anybody with much criminal practice, so that was my first assignment."

"What was your court appearance about?"

"Bailing out a client, or rather, somebody they hope will become a client."

"Who was that?"

"Can't talk about it."

"As you wish. Did he make bail?"

"He did, to the ADA's surprise. The judge wanted two

million, cash, and my client had it. Shocked the whole courtroom."

Stone frowned. "What was the charge?"

"Murder one."

Stone's jaw dropped. "And you got bail for that? How'd you do it?"

"I made the judge an offer he apparently couldn't refuse. He was too stunned to turn me down, and the ADA was speechless."

"How'd you come up with that number?"

"I thought that two mil had a nice ring to it. The judge thought so, too, I guess."

"Congratulations," Stone said. He was trying to decide what to say next when dinner was served, and he decided to talk about it later.

TWENTY-SIX

They dined on pâté Diana and moussaka, Greek dishes that Helene's mother had taught her, and apple tart for dessert. They moved to the sofa for coffee and cognac, and Stone thought they might as well get work out of the way as a subject.

"How did you come to have Edwin Charles Jr. as a client?"

"I thought that might come up."

"Care to answer the question?"

"I think I told you I had met him."

"Yes. Is that when he hired you?"

"No, someone else you don't know told him that I had joined Woodside & Weems, and he got somebody to call me. The firm was fine with me representing him. And they've promised that if I do a good job, they might broaden my role at the firm."

"Let me hazard a guess: the firm knew that his stepmother,

Annetta Charles, had dispensed with their services, and were replaced by Woodman & Weld, under my supervision."

"I believe that came up," she said.

"And someone suggested to you that, if you do a good job handling Junior, then they might take a step toward regaining his legal representation."

"That might have been mentioned, in passing."

"I'll bet. Well, you should know that I not only represent the estates of Edwin Sr. and Annetta, but that I am their executor, as well. Which means that, in order for Woodside & Weems to pry their way back into that particular piece of business, they would have to do such a convincing job, because, as executor, I would have to fire myself from the legal representation."

"I don't think it was put to me quite that way."

"I think I can promise you that will not happen."

"I understand."

"Good. Now there's no further reason for us to discuss work, is there? At least, until Eddie Jr. goes to trial."

"I suppose not."

"Good," Stone said. "Now, can I interest you in a more carnal subject?" He rubbed a knuckle lightly over a nipple and got a positive response.

"Oooh," she said. "That is an unfair tactic."

"I want you to know that both my nipples are available to you. Fair enough?"

She pinched one of his lightly. "Is this one fully operational?" she asked.

"They both are, and at your disposal."

"Well, then," she said.

There was a pause in the action while Fred took away their dishes, then an enthusiastic resumption. They could not bring themselves to leave the sofa, but their clothing did.

Much later, Bridget sat up. "I have an early meeting tomorrow morning," she said. "I should go."

"I wouldn't eject you into the storm," Stone said. "Just listen to that rain. We could move to the master suite, where I possess an alarm clock."

"I guess that will have to do. Anyway, I have a change of clothes in my bag."

"Clever girl," Stone said, picking up the bag and leading her upstairs, where the action resumed.

The next morning, Stone found Joan waiting in his office when he came downstairs. "Good morning," he said.

"Maybe not," Joan replied. "Eddie Jr. is out on bail."

"I heard."

"And he's waiting outside to see you."

"Kindly throw him out into the street."

"I heard that," a voice said. Stone looked up to find Eddie Jr. standing in the doorway.

"Oh, good. Then Joan won't have to explain it to you."

"I'm here about my trust."

That was legitimate business, Stone supposed. "Go ahead."

"Why is it I can get two million dollars from my trust as bail, but I can't get a hundred thousand for clothes and other necessities."

"Because the two million is in the hands of the court, not yours, and you can't spend it. By the way, have you read the conditions of your bail?"

"They're in my pocket."

"Yes, but have you read them?"

"It's on my list of things to do."

"Well, you'd better move it to the top of your list. Because if you violate one of them, even a little, like leaving New York City, you will be arrested and your two million will vanish in a puff of smoke. And by the way, the Hamptons are not located in New York City."

"That seems extreme."

"The court thinks of them as extremely reasonable. And if you violate that or any other of the rules, I will, as an officer of the court, be required to report it to the judge, who will not be understanding."

"You'd do that, wouldn't you?"

"Most certainly."

"Eddie," Joan said, "why don't you go lay your head wherever you're laying your head these days. After, of course, a shower and a scrub."

"I didn't like the plumbing facilities in jail," Eddie explained, "nor the company."

"Joan," Stone said. "If he's not in the street within thirty seconds, you have my permission, as an officer of the court, to shoot him."

"Sounds like fun," Joan said, propelling Eddie Jr. down the hallway toward the front door.

TWENTY-SEVEN

Stone called Dino.

"Bacchetti."

"I have info on Junior."

"Okay, shoot."

"If you'd like to lay hands on him, he's just left my office, headed for either the Athletic Club or the Yale Club."

"As it happens," Dino said, "I cannot lay hands on him for the murder charge, because he made bail."

"I think it may profit you to tail him, because he will almost certainly violate the terms of his bail. He thinks, for instance, that the Hamptons lie in this city."

"I can't violate him for leaving town. Get him to violate in the city, and I'm on him."

"We have only to wait," Stone said. "It would be handy if one or more of your people were present when he violates."

"My people have no psychic powers. And I have insufficient manpower at my disposal to make up for that shortcoming."

"Can you handle dinner?"

"I have a hankering for an Italian fish stew," Dino replied.

"Caravaggio, at seven," Stone said.

"I'll race you." Dino hung up.

Stone pretended to work for another hour, then the phone rang.

"Bridget on one," Joan said.

Stone punched the button. "Top o' the morning to you."

"You have a terrible Irish accent," she said.

"Thank you for pointing that out."

"I just wanted to thank you for a lovely dinner and a lovely the rest of it, too."

"Dino and I are feasting Italian this evening, at Caravaggio. Care to join us?"

"Does this mean I get two rolls in the hay, instead of just one?"

"Not unless we can exchange Dino for a suitable person of the female persuasion," Stone replied.

"Perhaps we can arrange that on another occasion soon. Meanwhile, I'll settle for being had just once this evening."

"I'm still recovering my health from the last one, but I may be able to rise to the occasion."

"I'll look forward to exploring that," she said. "What time?"

"Seven PM, Seventy-Third, just west of Madison."

"Done."

They both hung up.

Joan came into the office with a typed document. "You need to sign this for the judge, to the effect that Eddie's trust is good for his bail."

Stone signed. "How's your new house coming along?"

"Well, I've scoured it of everything of Aunt Annetta's that I hate. So it looks remarkably like a stylish person lives there."

"I'll bet it does."

"I was thinking of having a few people over for dinner soon, say Sunday evening? Will you come and bring a female person?"

"I would be delighted."

"There'll be a few people you know. It's black tie, six-thirty for drinks."

"Count on me."

TWENTY-EIGHT

Stone's car delivered them to the house at six-forty. The butler admitted them and showed them to the elevator, pressing the button for them.

They emerged into the living room that Stone had visited before, but a few flashy things had been removed, and there were large arrangements of fresh flowers scattered here and there.

Joan greeted them and was introduced to Bridget. Stone had never seen Joan dressed to kill, and he was impressed. A butler took their drinks order. "You look glorious," Stone said, "and so does the house."

"Thank you, thank you," Joan replied, obviously excited. The butler whispered something to her. "Oh, some special guests have arrived," she said. "Excuse me."

"Shall we circulate?" Bridget asked.

"Let's wait a minute and see who the special guests are."

"Are you likely to know them?"

"I know most of the people in this room, but let's wait and see." They took a position to one side of the elevator.

Shortly, the doors opened and five people stepped out. Stone knew two of them. "Mr. Mayor and Mrs. Shawn," Stone said. Of the other three people, two were detectives Stone knew and nodded to; the third was Edwin Charles Jr.

"This young fellow," the mayor said, indicating Eddie Jr., "was at the mansion for a drink, and we asked him to join us. I expect you know him."

"All too well," Stone said, not bothering to shake the outstretched hand. "In fact, his late stepmother, who was my client, took out a TRO, barring him from all of her homes."

"She's dead," Eddie protested.

"Nevertheless, we will respect her wishes." Stone gestured to the cops, and one of them stepped back onto the elevator, bumping Eddie ahead of him.

"I'm very sorry, Stone," the mayor said. "We had no idea."

"Not to worry, Mayor," Stone said. "He's a well-known party crasher."

Joan joined her guests. She whispered to Stone, "Did I see what's-his-name?"

"Here and gone," Stone said, then introduced Bridget to the mayor.

Others approached the mayor, so Stone and Bridget eased away.

"Ah, so we're manhandling my client into the elevator, now?"

"It was a brief encounter," Stone said. "He's barred from the premises."

"By whom? The late Mr. and Mrs. Charles?"

"By their executor," Stone replied, as a server delivered fresh drinks. "Do you want to see the TRO?"

"Yes, please."

"It'll have to wait until tomorrow. It's in my desk drawer. Besides, the police will already have shot him by now."

"For what cause?"

"Nothing special. He just brings that out in people."

A silver bell tinkled, and the crowd began looking for their place cards at one of the many tables awaiting them. Stone located theirs at the table with Joan and the mayor and his wife. Stone was seated between Mrs. Shawn and Joan.

"Thank you so much for ejecting that horrible little man," the mayor's wife said.

"You're very welcome," Stone said. "And I've never heard him described more aptly."

"He actually pushed his way into our car. The mayor is far too lenient with people like that. He kept telling us that you are his lawyer."

"You may rest assured," Stone said, "that that was a bald-faced lie." She turned to speak to someone else.

Joan nudged him. "I've remonstrated with the butler. He

was cowed by the presence of the mayor. What did you do with Eddie?"

"He's being buried on a construction site around the corner. Concrete will be poured."

"I'm so relieved," Joan said.

After dinner there was dancing, to the music of Peter Duchin, and Bridget caught up with Stone.

"Hi there, where were you seated?"

"In plain view of you, and I read lips."

"I'm sorry, but lip-reading is not admissible evidence in a court of law, unless the witness is a deaf-mute."

"You made that up!"

"Are you absolutely sure? I refer you to the criminal code."

"I'll bet there's a copy in the library here," she said.

"The previous owner would have had little use for it."

"You have an answer for everything, don't you!"

"Would you hire an attorney who didn't?"

TWENTY-NINE

Stone also danced with Joan, who was more fleet of foot than he had suspected, and with the mayor's wife, who liked dancing closer than Stone was comfortable with, in the circumstances.

He caught up with Bridget, who had been dancing with the mayor.

"The mayor doesn't like Eddie Jr., either. I think he pretended to just to annoy his wife."

"I wouldn't want her annoyed with me."

"You danced with her, didn't you?"

"Yes, and my crotch got a workout I hadn't expected."

"Maybe you should have found a pile of coats on a bed somewhere and taken advantage."

"Funny, she suggested that, too. Is that something you have in mind?"

"Yes, but on your bed and without the coats."

"I like the idea. Remind me later." He squeezed her hand. "Oh, shit."

"What's wrong?"

"I just spotted Eddie Jr. on the other side of the room." They strolled over to where one of the mayor's security detail was standing, ogling the female dancers.

"You removed Eddie Charles Jr. from the party, did you not?"

"I did, Mr. Barrington."

"Where did you dispose of the body?"

"Broadly speaking, in the gutter."

"He has arisen from the gutter and is groping an unsuspecting female guest across the room, due south."

"I'm on it," thc man said.

Stone held on to his sleeve for a moment. "Not too gently, but don't leave any marks. It might help if his tuxedo were too soiled for him to rejoin the party. It's still raining, so that shouldn't be too difficult."

"Got it," the man said, then hurried away. Stone watched as Junior disappeared down a hallway, between two large men.

"Is that settled?" Bridget asked

"It is, short of an early death." He found a sofa and a couple of brandies and sat her down. "Are you beginning to understand that Eddie Jr. would be an undesirable client for Woodside & Weems?"

"I am receiving that signal," she said.

"Do you think you might be able to explain that convincingly to your managing partner?"

"What words should I choose?"

"The phrase 'ticking time bomb' comes to mind," Stone said. "And you might mention that he is the *only* suspect in the murder of his stepmother."

"My problem is that I will have failed to use him to make rain. Warning them off isn't all that rewarding."

"To have saved your firm from a debacle ought to add some luster to your reputation. Don't worry, Eddie will prove your case. It's only a matter of time."

"I hope he hurries up," Bridget replied.

The cop reappeared at Stone's elbow. "Mission accomplished, I believe. It's storming out there, and the subject didn't have a raincoat or an umbrella, and he's missing a shoe. And, in the words of the immortal Johnny Mercer, 'no cabs to be had out there.'"

Stone tucked two hundreds into the cop's jacket pocket. "You fellas have a few on me," he said.

"At an appropriate moment," the cop replied.

"Have we tripped the light fantastic enough?" Stone asked Bridget.

"I certainly have."

"Then let's get out of here."

They took the elevator down to the garage where Fred and the Bentley were waiting and headed down Fifth Avenue. They had just turned the corner when Bridget tugged at Stone's sleeve. "Look," she said, nodding toward the sidewalk.

Stone looked. Standing in the gutter was Junior, looking

very much like a drowned rat, his thumb out to passing cars. "I don't think that even the kindest-hearted person would want someone that wet in his automobile," he said.

"Oh, it's not that long a walk to the Athletic Club."

"A lot farther to the Yale Club," Stone said.

THIRTY

When Stone got to his office the following morning, Joan was waiting for him. "Wonderful party last night," he said. "I never knew you were such a hostess."

"Thank you. I've had too few opportunities to show it," she replied. "My mother taught me well."

"I'll look forward to the next one. What's on this morning?"

"Do you know a Judge Fitzroy Barron?" she asked.

"Everybody knows him," Stone said, "though we've not met."

"Yes, you have. You shook his hand at the party last night."

"Oh God, and I didn't even recognize him?"

"He recognized you. He'd like you to come to see him at ten o'clock this morning. At 740 Park Avenue."

Stone looked at his watch. "Half an hour. Tell Fred to saddle the Bentley, while I change into a better suit."

Stone walked into the lobby of the fabled building, widely thought to be the finest residence in the city. He gave his name to the desk man and took the elevator upstairs. He was greeted by a butleresque figure in a black suit. "Mr. Barrington, please follow me." The man led him through two other rooms into a library that would have been at home in the depths of Harvard. The judge rose to greet him from a wing chair before the fire. "Mr. Barrington," he said, offering his hand.

"Judge Barron. I'm sorry I didn't get to spend more time with you last evening."

"That's all right. You seemed to be every woman's favorite dance partner, so how could I impose? Please have a seat. Coffee, or something stronger?"

"Strong coffee would suit me fine," Stone said, taking a chair. The butler must have anticipated him, for he appeared at Stone's elbow with a silver tray bearing a fine china cup of coffee. "Thank you, Judge."

"I'd like it if you'd call me Fitz," the elder man said. "There's too much formality in my life."

"Thank you, Fitz. And I'm Stone."

"I've followed your career with interest since you joined Woodman & Weld," he said.

Stone gulped.

"Oh, I know about all those cases nobody over there wants to talk about. We all handled a few of those in our extreme youth."

Stone couldn't imagine one of America's most distinguished

jurists handling those cases. Barron had retired from the Supreme Court at seventy-five, on principle, and he still seemed a vigorous man.

"Last night," the judge said, "I couldn't help noticing your handling of Edwin Charles Jr."

"I'm sorry you noticed, sir," Stone said. "It took me a couple of tries to get it right."

"Well, you didn't actually kill him," Barron replied, "and I imagine that required great restraint."

Stone chuckled. "Not that it didn't cross my mind."

"I sympathize. I'd like to shoot him between the eyes myself."

"Your numbers are legion, Fitz," he said, forcing himself to use that name.

"Is it true that you represent him?"

"It is not, sir. I am merely the appointed trustee of a trust set up for him by his stepmother, Annetta."

"Ah, Annetta," Barron said with a little smile. "We all remember her well."

Stone was afraid he knew what that meant. "So I hear. She asked me to draw up her will and to be the executor of hers and her husband's estates."

"So, you exercise some authority over Junior?"

"Only the authority, I fear, to control his withdrawals from his trust."

"Off the record, of course, do you think Junior murdered Annetta?"

Stone shrugged. "He had a motive, of course, or at least he thought he did."

"Oh? Did he inherit?"

"No. Annetta surgically removed that possibility when she signed her last will. Of course, Junior didn't know that at the time."

"You haven't answered my question," Barron said.

"I think it's a distinct possibility. Though, like the police, I can't prove it. Indeed, if it went to trial, I think a good lawyer might get him off, if he could impose a little courtroom decorum on his client."

"If that trial ever happens, I'd like a seat in the courtroom," Barron said. "Though not on the bench."

Stone finished his coffee, and the cup was immediately replenished by the butler.

"I'd like to retain you," Barron said.

Stone was surprised. "Oh?"

"I have a granddaughter who has been seeing rather too much of Junior."

"Oh," Stone replied. "My condolences."

"I'd like you to make him go away."

"Fitz," Stone said regretfully. "If I knew how to do that, he would already be gone."

"Quite," the judge said. "Nevertheless . . ."

"I have a friend who has a solution for problems like Eddie Jr.," Stone said.

"And what is his solution?"

"Shoot him in the head, and don't get caught."

The judge laughed aloud for a moment, then composed himself. "Nevertheless."

"I'd be grateful if you would complete that thought," Stone said, "because I can't complete it for you."

"I'm afraid I've imposed on your good nature, Stone—not to mention your ethical standards. I apologize."

"No offense taken, Fitz."

"I suggested a TRO to my granddaughter," Barron said.

"And?"

"She won't have it. She finds him too entertaining."

"I think that, after more exposure to him, she will find him a little less entertaining."

"I had thought that, too," Barron said. "But it hasn't worked out that way, and I'm afraid that waiting for it to work will require a great deal more patience than I possess."

"Si non nunc, quando?" Stone said.

"'If not now, when?' An excellent personal motto."

"Fitz, I'm still working on this problem, for my own mental health. If I find something that works, and won't get either of us arrested, I'll be in touch."

"I would be grateful to hear from you," Barron said.

Stone rose, thanked him for the coffee, wished him well, and then left.

THIRTY-ONE

When Stone returned to his office, Joan braced him. "How did that go?"

"Well, I've met somebody else who detests Junior," Stone said. "And he has a granddaughter who thinks Eddie is cute."

"Uh-oh. What was your solution to that problem?"

"I didn't offer him one."

"Pity. The judge's name would have looked good on your client list."

"I think the judge wants the matter handled without his fingerprints on it."

"You mean, he wants Eddie bumped off?"

"No, but I think it would cheer him up to see such a crime on the front page of a newspaper."

The phone rang, and Joan answered. "Dino for you on one."

"Morning, Commissioner."

"Pretty good party last night, huh?"

"Better than pretty good."

"Dinner at Clarke's, seven?"

"Sold. See you there." They both hung up.

Stone found Dino at the bar at Clarke's, halfway through his first Scotch.

"Did you run into Judge Fitzroy Barron at the party last night?" Dino asked.

"Yes, but I didn't remember, until he called this morning and invited—well, practically ordered that I show up at his apartment."

"Did you?"

"Of course. A lawyer doesn't turn down a meet with a former Supreme Court justice."

"What did he want with you?"

"He seemed to want me to strangle Eddie Charles Jr. while he watched."

"Well, to know Junior is to hate his guts. What is Barron's beef with him?"

"He's been paying too much attention to the judge's granddaughter, who is encouraging the attention."

"Eddie has a real gift for getting up people's noses, doesn't he?"

"So far, I haven't met anyone who enjoys his company. Makes me wonder about the granddaughter."

"How many times did you have him thrown out of the party last night?"

"Only twice. The second one stuck. We saw him trying to hitchhike down Fifth Avenue when we left, and he was missing a shoe."

"Not a night for hitchhiking."

"Not even if you have a raincoat and an umbrella. And two shoes."

"Do you think the kid is some kind of mental case?"

"That's a good possibility."

"Why don't you send him to a good shrink?"

"I don't think a shrink could handle Eddie any better than anybody else," Stone said. "He'd probably just toss him out a window during their first session."

"Any chance of getting him committed?"

Stone shook his head. "I think he can feign sanity long enough to avoid a straitjacket."

"No custodial care, huh?"

"You have a better chance of arranging that than I do," Stone said. "Convict the son of a bitch for murder one and let the State of New York prison system deal with him."

"Nah, lawyers like you will keep him on the street."

"You know, Fitzroy Barron all but invited me to have the kid professionally hit."

"In so many words?"

"Of course not, dummy. Don't you think he's lawyer enough to suggest that without suggesting that?"

"I suppose he must be."

"Trust me. I was a little annoyed that he would pick me to

arrange it. He'd apparently heard some stories about how I handled things for Woodman & Weld in my early days there."

"Were you arranging a lot of hits then?"

"Of course not. I've never done anything like that."

"Well, it's interesting to think that old Fitz would think you have."

"Yeah, I wonder who he's been talking to." He looked at Dino narrowly.

"Don't point that thing at me!" Dino protested. "I don't even know Judge Barron, apart from shaking his hand last night."

"He should have talked to you," Stone said. "You probably know a dozen cops who would take that contract."

"No, I got rid of those sorts of cops early in my reign."

"Your *reign*? You think they look upon you as a king?"

"They'd fucking well better, unless they want to serve out their twenty years in uniform in the nether reaches of the Bronx."

The maître d' caught Stone's eye and motioned him toward the back room, where he had a good table for them. They ordered steaks, as usual, and a decent bottle of red.

"Did you find a murder weapon in the Charles case?" Stone asked Dino.

"Funny you should mention that," Dino said. "No, as it happens."

"Has Eddie Jr. got a firearm registered in his name?"

"You don't think we would have checked?"

"Can I take that as a no?"

"Yes," Dino replied.

"What was the weapon?"

"A .38."

"Did you get a good slug out of Annetta?"

"Yeah, we did."

"Did you search Eddie's digs?"

"At the Yale Club? Of course."

"How about at the Athletic Club?"

"Damn it, we only searched the one."

"Well, he's been sleeping on and off at both."

"Well, shit," Dino said, getting out his phone and delivering some terse instructions about a search warrant.

THIRTY-TWO

Stone came down to his office the following morning with a word from the crossword still on his mind. He looked around for his *Concise Oxford English Dictionary* but couldn't find it. Normally, it was within reach of his chair.

He buzzed Joan.

"Yes, boss?"

"Have you borrowed my *Concise Oxford*?"

"Is that the small one?"

"Yes."

"No, but you've got all twenty volumes of the big one right there."

"Every time I pick up one of those volumes, I pull a muscle."

"I'll have a look around for the *Concise Oxford*."

"Good."

Joan came into his office half an hour later and handed him the *Concise Oxford*. "There you go."

"Thanks, where'd you find it?"

"I didn't, Helene did."

"Okay, where'd Helene find it?"

"You know those two guest rooms that you turned into a suite for Peter when he came to live here?"

"Yes."

"There." She started out of the room.

"Wait a minute."

Joan stopped.

"How'd my *Concise Oxford* get into Peter's suite? I use it every day, and I haven't been in that suite for, what, a year? And Peter stays at the Carlyle now, when he visits."

"Beats me." She placed a hand on the book. "You want me to slap it around until it talks?"

"Oh, never mind." He snatched the book away.

Stone set the dictionary on his desk and went upstairs to Peter's suite. It was in perfect order. He walked around the two rooms and looked in the bedroom closet. There were a half dozen suits and jackets hanging there. Well, he said to himself, I guess Peter keeps a few things here for when he visits, even if he doesn't visit anymore. He went back down to his office and sat down, staring at the beautifully bound book; he had bought it in London many years ago. The way the light caught it, he could see a partial fingerprint on the leather. He thought about that for a minute, then he scribbled a note and stuck it inside the cover, gingerly dropped the dictionary into a book mailer, and buzzed for Joan.

"What's up, boss?"

"Are you going to go on calling me that? You're richer than I am, for God's sake."

"Habit," she said.

He handed her the book envelope. "Will you messenger this down to Dino for me, please?"

"Doesn't the police commissioner have a dictionary?"

"I expect so. I just want him to run the fingerprints."

"What fingerprints?"

"The ones on the dictionary."

"I'll save me the trouble," she said, "you'll find mine, yours, and Helene's. Maybe Peter's, if fingerprints last that long."

"Humor me, please."

She picked up the package and flounced out of his office.

"And don't flounce!" he called after her.

"Why not?" she called back. "I'm richer than you!"

Stone massaged his temples and the back of his neck.

He was just finishing his lunch when Dino called.

"Hi there."

"Hi there, my ass. Why are you making work for me?"

"What?"

"Your fucking dictionary!"

"Work?"

"Didn't you send it to me to check for prints?"

"Oh, yes, I forgot."

"It's so unimportant that you forgot about it?"

"Not on purpose."

"What did you want to know?"

"I wanted to know whose prints are on it."

"What the fuck for? Was it stolen?"

"No, it was just somewhere in the house where it shouldn't have been, and I want to know who handled it."

Dino made a muttering sound. "Like we don't have enough to do. You have to make work for us."

"I didn't make the work. Somebody else did."

"Who?"

"That's what I want to know from the prints."

"So you want your police department to figure it out?"

"Yes, please. If you have a moment."

"All right, I've got a list right here. Ready? You want to write these down?"

"Just read them to me. I can remember them."

"Okay: yours, Joan's, Helene's, and Eddie Charles Jr.'s."

"What?"

"I asked you to write them down!"

"Was Junior's name on that list?"

"I read it out loud. Are you going deaf?"

"What are Eddie's prints doing on my dictionary that never leaves my desk?"

"So now you want me to open a case on your dictionary?"

"No, no, Dino, just messenger it back to me."

"You sure you don't want it tested for bloodstains or DNA?"

"No, no, thanks for your trouble, Dino."

"No trouble," Dino said, then hung up.

Stone buzzed Joan.

"Yes, boss?"

"Can you come in here for a minute, please?"

"Be right there." Joan materialized in the doorway. "Yes, sir?"

"Guess whose fingerprints are on my dictionary?"

"Okay: yours, mine, and Helene's."

"You missed one."

"Who?"

"Eddie Jr.'s."

"Don't be ridiculous," she said, then went back to her office.

"I'm going to get to the bottom of this!" he shouted.

"You do that!" she shouted back. "Let me know what you find when you get there!"

THIRTY-THREE

Stone thought about it, then buzzed Joan again.

"Yes, sir?" she said wearily.

"I want you and Helene to go up to Peter's suite together and make an inventory of everything in it."

"Everything?"

"Well, not everything. Just any items that aren't Peter's."

"How will we know which ones those are?"

"Helene will know. And I want to know the last time she cleaned the room."

"All right." Joan sighed. She hung up.

Twenty minutes later, Joan buzzed.

"That was fast."

"We didn't have to go very far."

"What?"

"The suits in the closet had a tailor's label, and inside that was the name of who it was made for. They were all made for Eddie Jr."

"Aha!" Stone shouted. "Is there a suitcase there?"

"Yes, with his luggage tag on it."

"All right, I want you to pack everything you think belongs to Eddie and take it out of here when you go home tonight."

"Then what?"

"Then give the suitcase to your butler and tell him to store it. Then figure out how Eddie got a key to my house."

"I think I've already figured that out," she said sheepishly.

"How?"

"I had new keys made, and I put them in the desk drawer in the library at my house. There's one missing, and Eddie must have it."

"Okay. When you're done packing, go to the alarm master control and change the password for entry." He gave her a new password. "Then tell everybody who should know what the new code is."

"Okay."

"And if you see Eddie, get my key back from him, as well as your house key. Shoot him, if you have to."

"I'd love to shoot him," she said. "Can I shoot to kill?"

"No, too much paperwork. Just scare the shit out of him."

A few minute later, Joan walked past his office and held up Eddie's suitcase for him to see.

"Jesus, it's alligator! Remind me, we did cut his allowance in half until we get his bail back, right?"

"We certainly did." She moved on to her office. Shortly, she buzzed Stone.

"Yes?"

"Dino for you on one."

"I nailed the bastard," Stone said.

"Which bastard?"

"Eddie Jr. We found some of his clothes in Peter's suite. The son of a bitch has been living here!"

"That would explain why he's been so hard to find," Dino said. "He wasn't at the Athletic Club, either, and we've run out of clubs he belongs to."

"Well, I can tell you, he doesn't belong to *this* club anymore."

"Dinner, Clarke's, seven?"

"You're on." They both hung up.

Stone got there first and ordered drinks for both of them. He had drunk half his bourbon before Dino showed.

Dino held the Scotch up to the light. "There's a layer of dust on my drink," he said.

"Next time, don't be late, and you'll have no dust problems," Stone replied.

"Why are you so grouchy tonight?" Dino asked.

"It's Eddie Jr. He's driving me nuts. Can you think of some reason to arrest him?"

"I tried that, but you got him bailed out."

"Oh, yeah. I did, didn't I? My mistake."

"Has he violated the terms of his bail?"

"I don't know. Is living in my house without my knowledge or permission a violation of his bail?"

"I don't think so," Dino said. "If you could find him in possession of a .38 pistol, that would do it."

"Next time I see him, I'll frisk him."

"When will that be?"

"If I'm lucky, never."

"And if you're not lucky?"

Stone smiled a little. "Look behind you."

Dino turned. "Hello, Eddie," he said. "What are you doing here?"

"Stone changed the code on his alarm, and I nearly got arrested."

"Close, but no cigar," Dino said.

"Stone, what's the new code?" Eddie asked, as if he expected to be told.

"None of your fucking business," Stone said, "and if you enter my house again, without my permission, I'll have Dino arrest you for breaking and entering."

"There's no breaking," Eddie said, holding up a key. "I've got a key."

Stone snatched it from him. "Not anymore," he said.

"Where am I going to sleep?"

"Try the gutter."

"You want me to sleep in the gutter?"

"I don't care where you sleep, as long as it's not in my house. Try Central Park. I hear the benches are nice there."

"That's very inhospitable of you," Eddie said.

"It is, isn't it," Stone replied, smiling. "It's very satisfying, too."

"Try the Y," Dino said.

"What's that?" Eddie asked.

"The YMCA. Heard of that?"

"No. What do the letters mean?"

"Young Men's Christian Association, I believe," Stone replied for Dino.

"I'm not a Christian, I'm a Buddhist."

"Don't worry, Christians are very tolerant about such things."

"Eddie," Dino said, "it's cheap, clean, and you'll make new friends. I think they have a pool, too."

"It probably stinks of chlorine. Where is it?"

Stone spoke up. "Just get into a cab and tell the driver to take you to the nearest Y." He handed Eddie ten dollars. "Here's cab fare. Remember not to write."

To Stone's surprise, Eddie left. He and Dino went into the dining room for dinner.

"What a pain in the ass that guy is," Dino said.

"You're finally getting the picture," Stone replied.

THIRTY-FOUR

Stone and Dino, after the departure of Eddie Jr., settled into their evening, enjoying their steaks and wine, and topping it all off with snifters of cognac.

"I can't tell you how relaxing it is to be rid of Junior," Stone said.

"Yeah, I haven't seen you this loose since he came into the picture. Maybe he's found a home at the Y," Dino suggested.

"God, I hope so."

Dino's phone rang, and he glanced at it. "I have to take this," he said. "I left instructions." He punched the button. "Bacchetti. Yeah? Yeah, that's right. Hang on." He covered his phone. "Eddie got into a fight with two other guys at the Y. Something about a blanket. They're holding him at the precinct. What do you want to do?"

Stone sighed. "Nothing. I want to do nothing."

"You want to just leave him there for the night?"

"How much will it cost to have them keep him forever?"

"He'll see a judge in the morning and probably get kicked into the street."

"Perfect," Stone said. "Let's let him live with the consequences of his actions."

"And it was all going so well," Dino said.

"It's still going well," Stone replied. "He can't get at me from jail, and he's already used his phone call. At least, he's going right past me now and straight to the top, which is you."

"I put out a call to be notified if he got arrested anywhere."

Stone's phone rang. "Yes?"

"It's Joan. I just got a message from Eddie. He's in jail. And having already used his phone call, presumably to call you, he got his cellmate to call me, and he told me to call you."

"That's all terribly interesting, Joan, but nothing to do with me—or, for that matter, you."

"So, I should just ignore the call?"

"That's what I would do."

"Then I'm going back to bed. Good night."

"Good night."

Stone hung up. "He got somebody to call Joan."

"He's like that bunny on TV," Dino said. "He just keeps on going."

Stone's phone rang, and he looked at the caller ID. "Call from somebody I never heard of."

"You know what that's about, don't you? Just shut down your phone until tomorrow morning."

"Good idea."

"Lawyers don't get calls in the middle of the night like cops and doctors."

"Actually . . ." Stone switched his phone back on. "We do sometimes. And those calls can be lucrative when they come in the middle of the night."

Stone got home after midnight, only slightly the worse for wear, and the office line was ringing. "Hello?"

"Is this the Barrington law firm?"

"It is."

"This is Sergeant Nolan at the precinct. I got an Edwin Charles Jr., says he's your client."

"Hmmm, let's see," Stone said. "Nope, he's not ours. Give him to a public defender."

"He won't take a PD."

"Then give him a cell. Put him in the tank with all the thieves and junkies."

"Whatever you say." He hung up, and Stone went to bed. Then, in the wee hours, his phone rang again. This one would be from night court, he knew. He picked up the phone. "Wrong number," he said, and hung up.

He remained at peace until Joan got in and rang him at his desk the following morning.

"Morning," she said cheerfully. "How many calls did you get last night either from or about Eddie?"

"Including this one? Eighteen—no, nineteen."

"It makes me sorry his parents showed him how to use a phone," she said.

"Why are you telling me this?"

"Oh, the reason I called is that there was a call from Bridget on the machine." She gave him the number.

"Thank you." He called Bridget. "I'm sorry, I just got your message," he said. "When did you get in?"

"Around two," she said. "The phone was ringing, and I thought it was you, so I answered."

"It wasn't me."

"No, it was the bailiff at night court. Eddie Jr. told them I was his lawyer, so I had to go down there and make bail for him."

"Oh God, how much?"

"Only five hundred. I had that in my ready bag."

"Where is the schmuck?"

"Out wandering the streets, I guess."

"Sweetheart, I'm so sorry about that. Tell you what, I'll buy you a great dinner this evening."

"Deal."

"My house at six-thirty?"

"Done." She hung up.

THIRTY-FIVE

Stone answered the front doorbell, first checking the viewing screen to make sure it wasn't Eddie.

"It is I," Bridget said. Stone buzzed her in.

"Come to the study," he said. They met there and embraced.

"Before I forget," Stone said. "Here's a check for Eddie's bail and your fee for representing him. It's from his trust."

"Thank you so much, and I have something for you," she said, handing him an envelope.

Stone found a check for two million dollars from the court, made out to Eddie's trust. "Holy mackerel!"

"I got the DA to cut him loose," she said. "Lack of evidence to convict. Same on the lesser charge."

"On behalf of Eddie's trust, I thank you," Stone replied. "Also, Eddie is now free of his bail restrictions and can leave town."

"Yes, he can."

Stone poured them both a gimlet, and they drank to Eddie leaving town. "Now," he said, "how can I actually get him to leave?"

The doorbell rang again, and Stone answered it from the study. A seedy-looking man stood at the door. "Yes?"

"I want Eddie," he said.

"Sorry, no Eddie at this address."

"He said you'd say that."

"He was right. Good evening." Stone sat down with his drink. The doorbell rang again, and Stone glanced at the screen. Same guy. Stone buzzed Fred Flicker on the intercom.

"Yes, Mr. Barrington?"

"Fred," Stone said, "there's someone at the door wanting Eddie, and even though I've told him no Eddie lives here, he keeps ringing the bell. Will you go and persuade him that no Eddie lives here, please?"

"Of course, Mr. Barrington."

"That guy looked pretty big," Bridget said. "Do you think Fred can handle him?"

"Don't be misled by Fred's small stature," Stone said. "He's an ex-Royal Marine commando."

"Still . . ."

Stone switched on the screen again. "Let's watch." He used a remote control to switch on the TV, giving them a wider camera angle.

"Yes?" Fred said.

"I'm looking for Eddie."

"There is no Eddie here. Look elsewhere. You've been told twice now."

The man reached out as if to take hold of Fred, but the smaller man took hold of his fingers, turned them palm up and applied pressure, raising the man on his toes to relieve the pain. "There are two things you can do," Fred said. "You can look elsewhere for Eddie, or you can look elsewhere for Eddie with a broken hand. What will it be?"

"I'll look elsewhere," the man said, gasping. Fred backed him down the front steps to the sidewalk before releasing him. "Then do so. Now." The man hurried away.

"That was remarkable," Bridget said. "I want one of those."

"A Fred?"

"Yes, please. Where did you find him?"

"A French friend of mine sent him to me as a gift for one year of his service. In less than a month I made him a permanent hire. I don't think you'd find another Fred at an employment agency."

Eddie met the man around the corner. "Well, Mac? What happened?"

"A little man came to the door and persuaded me that you don't live there."

"That would be Fred."

"That will be twenty bucks," Mac said and stuck out his hand to receive the money.

Eddie paid him, because he had learned at the Y not to stiff guys like Mac.

"Anything else?"

"You still got that burner phone?" Eddie asked.

"Yeah."

"I'll be in touch."

"Get this straight," Mac said. "I'm not messing with that Fred guy."

"Got it." Eddie took out his cell phone and called Stone's cell.

"Yes?"

"It's Eddie."

"Oh, Eddie, I'm glad you called. I've got good news for you."

"Good news?"

"Your attorney has persuaded the DA to drop both charges against you, for lack of evidence. The court has restored your bail money to your trust, and your trust has paid your attorney's fee."

"Well, that is good news, Stone. Can we have dinner?"

"We cannot and will not, ever. You are now free to leave town, and you can't do it quick enough for me."

"But where will I go?"

"You can go back to the Hamptons, as long as you stay away from Annetta's house and don't get arrested for trespass. Or, you can go into any bookshop, buy a world atlas, then open it, close your eyes, and put your finger on the page. Keep doing that until your finger lands on a place that sounds appealing, then go there. Don't leave a forwarding address, because neither Joan nor I will be in touch. Is all that clear to you?"

"Well . . ."

"If you come back here, you will be met by Fred, and you don't want that."

"Well . . ."

"Bon voyage!" Stone shouted, then hung up.

"Nice speech," Bridget said. "Do you think it will register with him?"

"Who knows?" Stone said, reaching for her. "But it will do for tonight. We've got half an hour before dinner."

"Then let's think of something to do," she said.

THIRTY-SIX

Eddie went back to the Y with Mac, his buddy. "There's that thing you said you were going to teach me," he said to Mac.

"You mean how to pick a lock?"

"That's what I mean."

Mac took a pouch from his pocket and unzipped it. "You'll need a set of these," he said.

"Where do I get a set of those?"

Mac grinned. "From me, of course."

"How much?"

"Two hundred bucks."

"I'll give you a hundred."

"One seventy-five or get them somewhere else."

"And that includes instruction?"

"That's another twenty-five."

"Oh, all right."

They began by taking apart the lock on the door to their

room so Mac could show Eddie how it worked. They moved on to a more challenging lock on the weight room door, then tried another. A couple of hours later, Eddie was picking locks. He packed a bag.

"Where you going?" Mac asked.

"Out of town."

"Without me?"

"I got all I need from you."

"You won't survive a day on the street without me."

Eddie thought about that. "Have you got any decent clothes?"

"I got a blue blazer and some khakis. Those'll work for me just about anywhere."

"Get packed," Eddie said.

Mac started packing.

"You know anything about cars?" Eddie asked.

"I know how to drive 'em and fix 'em. Why?"

"I want to buy one."

"What kind?"

"A Mercedes."

"You got a hundred grand?"

"A used Mercedes."

"Let's check the want ads."

Joan knocked on Stone's door.

"What can I do for you?"

"I want to take a couple of days off."

"Sure. You going out of town?"

"I thought I'd take a look at Annetta's place in the Hamptons."

"Going alone?"

"I thought I'd ask my friend Betty," she said.

"Taking the train?"

"I own three cars, remember?"

"Oh, right. Sure, take the time."

"You can reach me on my cell," she said. "It'll be almost like having me here."

"I'll manage."

"Yeah, sure," she muttered to herself. "See you soon."

Eddie left town in a four-year-old Mercedes station wagon with only thirty thousand miles on the odometer. He and Mac drove the Long Island Expressway to the end, then used the GPS to guide them.

"What's the address?" Mac asked.

"Further Lane, East Hampton."

"What number?"

"I'll know it when I see it."

Mac entered Further Lane into the GPS. "We're off and running," he said.

By mid-afternoon they were in East Hampton. They picked up some groceries and drove to Further Lane. "That one," Eddie said as they drove past.

"You want to wait until dark?" Mac asked.

"Nah, we can park where the car won't be seen from the street." Eddie made a left turn and drove into the driveway.

"Very nice," Mac said. "Is there a security system?"

"What if there is?"

"I might be able to deal with it, if it's one I know."

Eddie pulled into a parking spot. "Okay, deal with it."

Joan and her friend Betty left Joan's new house in Annetta's Mercedes-Benz S550 convertible. "Pretty snazzy car," Betty said.

"If you're inheriting, why not go for snazzy?"

"I can't argue with that."

Joan headed for the LIE.

Mac got them into the house without setting off any alarms, and they unloaded their things and the groceries.

"You cooking?" Mac asked doubtfully.

"Nah, let's go into the village and get something. There are restaurants still open, off season."

"As long as you're buying," Mac said.

"I'm buying," Eddie replied. His trust fund was working again, and he had plenty of cash, a credit card, and a checkbook.

They got into the car and drove away. As they turned toward the village, another Mercedes, a convertible, passed them going the other way.

"I guess a Mercedes is pretty good camouflage out here," Mac said.

"Yep. One thing, Mac."

"What's that?"

"We don't want to get into any scrapes out here. We want to fit in. The cops don't bother you when you fit in."

"Does my blazer look okay?"

"Yeah, everything works, except your haircut."

"What's wrong with it?"

"Grow some hair."

"Right away?"

"As soon as possible."

Joan pulled into the driveway. "There's a light on in the kitchen," she said. "One upstairs, too."

"The maid, maybe?"

"She doesn't come until the first of the week."

"She must have left it on the last time she was here."

Joan put the car in the garage, and they carried their things inside.

"Wow!" Betty said, looking around. "I've always wanted a friend with a house like this."

"Well, now you've got one."

"Pity you're not an eligible bachelor."

"You had one of those, and you divorced him," Joan said.

Betty looked in the fridge. "There's eggs, bacon, and orange juice here," she said.

"I'd better speak to the maid when she comes back," Joan replied.

THIRTY-SEVEN

Eddie and Mac finished their steaks, had a couple more drinks, then drove back to Further Lane.

"There are more lights on than when we left," Mac said.

"They're on a timer," Eddie replied. "Keeps guys like you away."

"Let's go in easy," Mac said. "These people could have a shotgun or something."

"Maybe we just give it a pass," Eddie said. "Go to a hotel."

"Nah," Mac said. "You just stay behind me. I'll handle it."

"Wait a minute, Mac . . ."

But Mac was already through the kitchen door. "Just stay behind me." He drew a pistol from his jacket pocket.

"Where the hell did you get a gun?" Eddie asked.

"From your sock drawer," Mac replied. "Shhhh." He walked

into the kitchen, looked around, then walked over to the bottom of the stairs. "Somebody's up there," he whispered.

"Mac, let's get out of here!" Eddie whispered.

"Listen, you, down there!" A woman's voice called out. "I'm armed. You leave the house right now, or I'm going to use it!"

Eddie froze in his tracks, but Mac was slowly climbing the stairs, the pistol held out in front of him. "If you've got a gun, you'd better drop it and come down here right now," Mac yelled. "I'm not kidding!" He kept climbing, and Eddie lost sight of him.

"Freeze!" the woman yelled. "Or I'll fire!"

"Yeah, sure, lady. You just come down here and be nice to me, and everything will be all right!"

Eddie took a few steps forward, until he could see Mac's feet. Then there came a roar from above, and Mac flew backward down the stairs, firing his gun at the wall.

Eddie didn't hesitate. He turned and ran out the back door, got the station wagon started, backed out of his space, and gunned it down the driveway. He checked the rearview mirror, but nobody was following him. The house disappeared behind the trees. He reached Further Lane, turned left, and drove fast. There were no lights on in the houses, and no cars in sight. He slowed to a more legal speed. He didn't need any tickets tonight. He made his way to the Long Island Expressway, set the cruise control to the speed limit, and concentrated on keeping the car in the correct lane.

He took deep breaths and, gradually, his trembling stopped, and he began to feel normal again.

Joan switched on the lights and looked down the stairs. She could see the bottoms of a pair of shoes. And as she crept down the stairs, her .45 held out in front of her, she saw the rest of him. His chest was a mess, and a couple of steps below him, a chrome, short-barreled pistol lay there, cocked. She edged her way past the man, watching for any signs of movement. His eyes were open, and there was an expression of mild surprise on his face, but he did not move or breathe. She reached the bottom of the stairs, went into the living room, turned on a lamp, picked up a phone, and called 911.

"East Hampton Police, Sergeant Bell speaking," a woman's voice said. "What is your emergency?"

"My name is Joan Robertson. I'm at the Charles home on Further Lane. There is an armed man in the house, and he has been shot in the chest. Please send police and an ambulance."

"We know the house, Ms. Robertson," the sergeant said. "Do you know if the man is dead?"

"He doesn't appear to be breathing, and his eyes are open."

"Someone will be right there."

"Thank you." Joan hung up and called another number.

"Hello," a sleepy voice said.

"It's Joan. I'm at the East Hampton house, and I just shot a man. I think he's dead."

"Hang up, call 911, then call me back. I'm getting dressed."

"I've already called 911. They're on their way."

"Are you hurt in any way?"

"No, I'm fine. I'm just scared."

"Okay, I'm going to try to get a chopper out there. What's the address?"

She gave it to him.

"Turn on all the lights, inside and out."

"There's a big lawn," Joan said, "on the street side of the house."

They both hung up, and Stone called Mike Freeman.

"Yes?"

"Mike, it's Stone. Joan has shot an intruder in her house in East Hampton. Can you get a chopper to pick me up at the East Side Heliport and get me out there?"

"Sure I can. What's the address?"

"It's on Further Lane. All the lights, inside and out, will be on."

"Get to the heliport," Mike said. "I've got a pilot on duty." He hung up.

Stone looked at his watch: 1:10 AM. He started dressing, then buzzed Fred.

"Yes, sir?"

"Fred, I need you to drive me to the East Side Heliport right now."

"Five minutes, sir."

Stone didn't wait for the elevator. He ran down the stairs.

Joan sat on the living room sofa, trying to put events in order.

"Joan?" A voice from upstairs. Betty.

"I'm in the living room, Betty," she called back. "Come on down, and don't trip over the corpse on the stairs!"

Betty tiptoed into the living room, clutching her nightgown around her. "There's a corpse on the stairs," she said.

"I know. Don't worry, he won't bother you." Joan glanced at Betty. "You might want to get a robe on," she said. "You don't want to inflame some young police officer. They're on the way."

"Gotcha," Betty said, and she went upstairs for a robe.

THIRTY-EIGHT

As Joan sat on the sofa, she set her .45 on the cushion beside her and waited for the police. Shortly, a car turned up and flashing lights played across the ceiling. She got up and was at the front door by the time the bell rang. "Please come in," she said to the uniformed man and woman on the front porch. She switched on the master controls for the house and the exterior.

The officers both had their hands on their weapons. "Good evening, ma'am," the young man said. "Are you armed?"

"No," Joan replied, holding open the door. "My pistol is on the sofa there," she said, pointing.

The two officers entered. "Is there anyone else in the house?" he asked.

"There are two other people here: my houseguest, Betty, who is upstairs getting decent, and the man lying at the bottom of the stairs, around the corner. I'll show you." She led the two officers into the foyer and pointed at the large man wearing a large hole in his chest. "I'm sorry I can't introduce you, but I don't know his name."

Both officers approached him with their weapons drawn. The woman felt for a pulse at his neck and looked at his eyes to inspect the pupil. "He's dead," she said, holstering her weapon. "I've got a snub-nosed .38 on the other side of the body."

Another woman appeared at the top of the stairs, wearing a silk dressing gown. "Good evening," she said.

"Betty," Joan said, "would you bring my handbag down here, please? Yours, too." Betty went back for the two bags.

"Let's all go into the living room and have a chat," the officer said when Betty returned with Joan's bag and her own. "I'm Sergeant Dave Powell, and this is my partner, Sergeant Florence Stern. She likes to be called Flo."

"How do you do?" Joan and Betty said in unison. They followed the officers into the living room.

Powell took a ballpoint pen from his shirt pocket, stuck it into the barrel of the .45, and dropped the gun into a zippered plastic bag.

"The only fingerprints you'll find on it," Joan said, "are mine. I cleaned it thoroughly when I was packing."

"Does it belong to you?" Powell asked.

"Yes, it's registered in my name: Joan Robertson."

"And do you have a permit for it?"

"Yes, full carry. May I get my ID from my bag?"

"Of course."

Joan produced her documents relating to the gun and her driver's license. "You, too, Betty," she said, and Betty produced her license.

"Now," Powell said, "I'd like you to answer some questions."

"If you'll forgive me, I'd rather wait for the arrival of my attorney. He will be here shortly."

"Local attorney?"

"From the city. He's coming by helicopter."

"As you wish, Ms. Robertson." They all sat quietly and waited. Another twenty minutes passed, then they could hear the helicopter's rotors beating against the air. The machine set down on the front lawn, and the pilot killed the engine.

"Excuse me," Joan said, and went to open the front door. Stone Barrington entered and looked around.

"Stone, these are Sergeants Dave Powell and Flo Stern. Sergeants, this is my attorney, Stone Barrington, of the firm of Woodman & Weld."

Stone looked at his watch. "Good morning," he said. "Would you mind if I have a moment alone with my client?"

"Of course not," Powell replied.

"Where's the body?" Stone asked Joan.

"Right this way," she replied. Stone walked around the body and satisfied himself that it wasn't going to walk away. Joan gave him a calm, clear account of the events of the evening and pointed out the pistol on the floor, then they returned to the living room.

"Sergeants, my client will be happy to answer your questions," Stone said. "I should point out that I do not represent Ms. Brower."

"I'd like you to," Betty said, "if that's all right."

"Yes, it is. Now you may both answer the officers' questions. Tell the truth, and don't leave anything out," Stone said to the women. He took a seat and listened quietly to the questions and answers.

There were noises of other vehicles at the front of the house. "That will be the ambulance, the medical examiner, and the crime scene team," Powell said. "Mr. Barrington, do you have any questions?"

"Just to repeat," Stone said. "Joan, Betty, do either of you know the intruder, or have you ever seen him before tonight?"

"No," they both said simultaneously.

"One more question. Does the pistol next to the body belong to either of you, or have either of you ever seen it before?"

They shook their heads. "No," Joan said. "He seems to have brought it with him."

"Sergeant Powell," Stone said, "will you please give Ms. Robertson a receipt for her weapon?"

"Of course," Powell said, and wrote one out on a page from his notebook.

"Sergeants, may we agree that what we have here is a routine B and E, and that Ms. Robertson fired her weapon in self-defense?"

"That appears to be the case," Powell said, "but that could change with further investigation."

"I don't think so," Stone said, standing up. "Joan, do you or Betty need transportation to the city?"

They both declined. "I have my car," Joan said.

"Sergeant Powell," Stone said, handing him a card. "Will you please forward a photograph of the weapon and any reports relating to ballistics tests to me? I'd like to have my own people take a look at those."

"Yes, Mr. Barrington."

Stone kissed both women good night, told them to go back to bed, then returned to the waiting helicopter.

He was back at the East Side Heliport before the intruder was on a slab.

THIRTY-NINE

It was daylight before Stone got back to his house, and he went back to sleep for another four hours. By the time he was dressed for the day, he had tried to flush his brain of the East Hampton business and failed. Joan and Betty had answered the questions of the police fully and completely, but he had not done so. He wasn't positive, but he thought the corpse at the party may well have been the man who had rung his doorbell a few nights ago, asking for Eddie. He checked for the image on the front door camera, but it had not been saved by the system, not having been instructed to do that.

Dino rang. "I called early this morning but got no answer. I assumed you were fucking somebody and couldn't talk."

"I wish that were true, but it is not."

"Then where were you?"

"In East Hampton, or on the way back by helicopter."

"Why didn't I know you were going to East Hampton?"

"Because I didn't know myself until around one AM. Also, because, contrary to your belief, I do not tell you my every move."

"Wrong. I don't ask, but eventually you tell me everything. All I want to know now is why you were in East Hampton."

"I was answering a homicide call."

"Are you acting under the delusion that you are still a policeman and working in the East Hampton jurisdiction?"

"Joan and a friend of hers were staying at the house she inherited from Annetta Charles, and she shot and killed an intruder."

"And she called you, instead of 911?"

"She called 911, then me. Mike Freeman loaned me a chopper. And, on arrival, I ascertained that the corpse was, indeed, dead. Then I listened to the police question the two women, and the chopper brought me back."

"What was the outcome of all this action?"

"I suggested to the two cops attending that this was a routine B and E, and that Joan shot the man in self-defense. They did not disagree, so I got the hell out of there before they started to ask *me* any questions."

"What were you afraid they would ask you?"

"They asked if I recognized the corpse."

"And you said, 'No'?"

"Yes."

"And that was not true?"

"No. Sort of. He looked a little like a guy who came to my

house a few nights before, rang the bell, and asked for Eddie Jr. I could see him on my security system. It could have been the same guy. I told him to go away."

"You were fucking somebody at the time, weren't you?"

"Not yet."

"So I'm supposed to get you out of this?"

"Out of what?" Stone asked.

"Out of lying to the cops during a murder investigation."

"I didn't lie to them. I don't know if it was the same guy who came to my door."

"You want me to tell them that?"

"I don't want you to tell them anything."

"You want me to conceal evidence in a homicide investigation?"

"Why confuse the East Hampton cops?"

"What about the ballistics report? You want me to lose that or sit on it?"

"What are you talking about?"

"I'm talking about the East Hampton cop who was sitting on my doorstep when I got to my office this morning, with a S&W snub-nosed .38 in a plastic bag."

"I gave him my card and asked him to send me a copy of the ballistics report. I didn't mention your name."

"He came to us because his other choice was the state crime lab, which might take a month to produce a ballistics report for a small-town cop shop."

"Did you run it?"

"I did."

"And what did you tell the nice young cop from East Hampton?"

"Well, I learned two things from the report, but I only told him one of those."

"Which thing did you tell him?"

"I told him that the slug found in the wall was fired from the .38 in the plastic bag. That pleased him."

"And what was the thing you didn't tell him?"

"That the .38 in his plastic bag also fired the two slugs that our ME dug out of Annetta Charles's head."

Stone was stunned. "Holy shit."

"Well, yeah. When we ran the ballistics test, an alarm bell in our system went off, telling us that the weapon had been used in a previous crime."

"But you didn't tell the East Hampton cop that?"

"Manhattan is not his jurisdiction, and Annetta is not his case. I figured he didn't need to know. I mean, he didn't even notice that three slugs had been fired from the gun. They dug one out of the woodwork in the Further Lane house, and that's what we tested."

"How could they miss the other two empty casings in the cylinder?"

"Go figure. Dinner tonight? Clarke's at seven?"

"Yeah." They both hung up.

FORTY

Late in the day, Stone got a call. "Stone Barrington."

"Mr. Barrington, is it?"

"How'd you guess?"

"Well . . ."

"Is this Sergeant Powell from East Hampton?"

"Yes, it is. I'm surprised that you answered your own phone."

"My secretary is in East Hampton for a few days."

"Oh. And I thought you were just good friends."

"That, too. What can I do for you, Sergeant?"

"I wonder if I could ask your assistance?"

"In what?"

"In retrieving our pistol from the NYPD."

"*Your* pistol? How is it yours?"

"It was used in a crime in our jurisdiction."

"No, it was not. It was *fired* in your jurisdiction, and the person doing the firing is dead. And Ms. Robertson is not a criminal."

"I'm sorry, I misspoke."

"Did you send the pistol to the NYPD?"

"I hand delivered it," Powell said, "along with a written request for a ballistics report."

"And did they tell you when they'd be finished with it?"

"Yes, they said by the end of the week."

"I suggest that you call them at the end of the week."

"Well, yes, but I need it before then to make a presentation to our chief."

"Sergeant, I'm curious as to why you called me instead of the NYPD."

"Ms. Robertson tells me you are close to the commissioner, and that you might speak to him on my behalf."

"As it happens, I'm dining with him this evening, but once again, I don't understand your proprietary attitude toward the pistol. Did it ever occur to you that the NYPD might have a prior claim?"

"No, sir."

"Well, Sergeant Powell, if you had thoroughly examined the pistol, you would have learned that the cylinder contained three empty shell casings."

"How could you know that?"

"Because a machine at the NYPD let it be known that the weapon had been used in the commission of a prior crime—to wit, a murder—in the jurisdiction of Manhattan. So the NYPD is unlikely to surrender the pistol to you. The only crime the pistol committed in East Hampton was to fire a round into the woodwork of the Further Lane house." Stone thought he heard a gulp at the other end of the line.

"Then what should I do?"

"I would, if I were you, put the ballistics report into the case file, and if you make a presentation to your chief, tell him that the only crime committed in Further Lane was breaking and entering, that the perpetrator is dead, and that the NYPD has, quite properly, retained possession of the pistol. You might also tell him why."

There was a stunned silence at the other end of the line. "I don't think I can do that," he said finally.

"I don't think you have another choice," Stone said. "Is there anything else I can do for you?"

"You could speak to the commissioner on my behalf."

"If I did that, the only thing I would get from him would be a lecture on the facts of the case, the very one I have just given you."

"I'm sorry to have troubled you, Mr. Barrington," he said.

"Apology accepted. Good day." Stone hung up.

Stone arrived at P. J. Clarke's just as Dino's official SUV pulled up. They walked into the bar together, where their drinks were already being poured.

Dino downed half of his in a gulp.

"Long day?" Stone asked.

"No longer than usual, but just as annoying," Dino replied.

"Why don't you just retire to a beach somewhere?"

"And give up my car with the whooper and flashing lights? How would I get anywhere?"

"Well, there is that, I suppose."

"I'm not trading that for a beach and a drink with an umbrella in it."

"Your point is well taken."

"There's more on your mystery pistol," Dino said.

"Tell me."

"The kid cop from East Hampton called to say that an ID card of sorts had been found on the body of the dead guy."

"What kind of ID?"

"One with the name 'Mac' written on it."

"Just 'Mac'? And who issued the card?"

"The YMCA on the West Side."

"So now we've got a nexus with the Black Dog, Eddie Jr.!"

"Not so fast, my friend. They don't have any record of an Eddie Charles Jr. as a guest there."

Stone frowned. "How about a record of Mac's whole name?"

"Nope. It's not that easy to get lucky on this case."

"Fingerprints?"

"There you got lucky. John Joseph MacLean."

"Well, he had to have gotten the pistol from Eddie."

"Once again, not so fast. Mr. MacLean has done time for burglary and was skillful enough to have gotten nailed only once. He could have burgled the house and got interrupted by Annetta and desired to eliminate her as a witness. Or somebody else did and sold the gun to Mac."

"Somebody like Eddie Jr.?"

"Maybe, but prove it."

"That's your job, not mine."

"Oh, you've just been keeping your hand in, huh?"

"In a manner of speaking. Oh, I had a call from Sergeant Powell, too, asking me to get you to give his gun back."

"*His* gun?"

"I pointed out his error. He wants to show it off to his chief."

"Well, fuck his chief and the horse he rode in on."

"I predicted to him that something like that would be your reaction, thus saving you from having to deal with him again."

Dino drained his glass and signaled the bartender for a refill. "You know me so well," he said.

"I do?"

"No, the bartender does."

FORTY-ONE

Stone went down to work the following morning and was surprised to find Joan there, bustling around his office.

"I thought you were in East Hampton. What are you doing here?" Stone asked.

"Cleaning up after you," she said. "It's astonishing how big a mess you can make in such a short time."

"Do you feel fully restored by your holiday in the Hamptons?"

"Whatever restoration I was feeling was blown away by the man I blew away," she said, collapsing into a chair next to his desk.

"I can understand how that would upset you," Stone said. "Would it do any good for me to tell you that you behaved correctly. And if you hadn't shot him, he might have trashed your new house and shot you and Betty dead—after raping the two of you, of course."

"Don't bother, I've already told myself that a hundred times, and it didn't work."

"I recall another occasion where you used your .45 on a man in this office, to keep him from killing me. How'd you handle it then?"

"Pretty much the same way, with pretty much the same result."

"I don't remember you being unduly upset that time," Stone said.

"Oh, you were just too busy to notice."

"I'm sorry I didn't notice. I expect I was spending all my time being glad that I wasn't dead and being grateful to you."

"You said that at the time. Again, you're welcome."

"Well, I have a few residences around this country and Europe. Would you and your friend like to spend some time at one of them?"

"Thanks, but now Betty is afraid that I'll shoot her by accident. And the guy would still be dead, and it would still be me who made him that way."

"In that case, get your ass back to work and clean up this place. It's a mess!"

Joan let out a bitter laugh, then did as she was told.

Eddie Jr. let himself into the garage of the Charles mansion—now the Robertson House—with his remote control and parked the station wagon, which had been thoroughly washed and cleaned, in a distant corner. He partly unscrewed the light bulb illuminating that area, then he walked to the only staff bedroom at garage level and took twenty minutes to pick the lock. Quickly, he satisfied himself that the room was not occupied by a staff member. It was neat, clean, and spacious. He brought in his luggage and unpacked, then a moment later he stretched out on the sofa, switched on the TV, and was watching an early Hitchcock film, *The 39 Steps*, set on the Scottish moors. He was soon asleep, confident of not being disturbed.

On her lunch hour, Joan drove her Mercedes convertible back to what she was starting to think of as the Robertson House and parked in the garage. As she entered, her headlights came on automatically, and for a second illuminated a Mercedes station wagon. She parked her car in its usual space, next to the green Mercedes station wagon that had belonged to the Charleses, then walked over to the wagon she had just seen, which was a metallic beige. She tried the doors, but they were locked. The car was scrupulously clean, inside and out, which made her think that one of the staff had been driving it. She took the elevator to the main floor and found the butler.

"Geoffrey," she said to him, "who drives the beige Mercedes station wagon parked in the garage?"

"Mostly, I and Cook drive it and mostly to the grocery and hardware stores, but it's green, not beige."

"Well, now there are two Mercedes wagons parked in the garage, and one of them is beige. Look into it, will you? Perhaps one of the neighbors is taking advantage of our garage space."

"Yes, ma'am."

Joan went up to her study and stretched out on the chaise lounge, and Geoffrey found her there a few minutes later. "Ms. Robertson, neither I nor anyone else on staff knows anything about the beige station wagon, and none of our keys fit it." He handed her a slip of paper. "Here is the license number. Perhaps one of your police sources can learn the name of the owner."

"Thank you, Geoffrey." She tucked the number into her bra and attempted to doze off, but couldn't. Finally, she called Stone.

"Yes, Joan?"

"Something strange has happened."

"Uh-oh. What is it this time?"

"There is a strange, late-model Mercedes station wagon, color beige metallic, parked in my garage, and no one here has a key to it or knows anything else about it."

"Then one of your neighbors is usurping your garage space."

"Geoffrey looked into that; not so."

"Can you give me the license number?"

"I can," she said, consulting the paper in her bra.

"I'll get back to you."

Stone called Dino.

"Bacchetti."

"It's Stone. Can you run a plate for me?"

"In seconds," Dino said, and Stone read him the number.

"Got it," he said. He tapped the number into his computer.

"Who owns it?"

"A Delaware corporation. Registered a week ago."

"Well, shit," Stone said, knowing how impossible it would be to trace that.

"A neighbor's, maybe?"

"They've already excluded that possibility."

"Well, whatever branch of the tooth-fairy organization that handles Mercedeses has just dropped one in Joan's garage. Congratulate her for me, will you?" He hung up.

Stone hung up and called Bob Cantor.

FORTY-TWO

Cantor answered on the first ring. "Speak to me."

"It's Stone Barrington, Bob. I wonder if you could solve a mystery for me."

"Tell me your mystery, and I'll see."

Stone explained.

"Did you run the VIN, the vehicle identification number?"

"Joan didn't think of that," Stone said.

"We're not going to get anywhere without it, unless I run down to Wilmington and ransack the State of Delaware's files."

"I'll get back to you."

Joan, who had just returned to Stone's house, helpfully walked into his office and handed him a piece of paper. "I thought the VIN might be helpful," she said.

"It would have been helpful the first time," Stone replied. "Call Bob Cantor and give it to him."

"Will do." She left his office.

Bob Cantor called half an hour later. "Got something on the Mercedes for you."

"Hit me with it."

"Nothing on the current owner, but I've got the previous owner's name and address, on the Upper West Side."

"See if you can run it down," Stone said. "Don't worry, you're on the clock."

"Certainly."

It was near the end of the workday when Cantor called back. "I called the previous owner, but she was hard of hearing, and I couldn't carry on a conversation with her. So I went up to her apartment, which is in a very posh apartment house on Central Park West, and shouted in her ear."

"And what was her response?"

"She was going to trade in the car on a new one, but she didn't like the dealer's offer for her car, so she ran a for sale ad in the *Times*. A young man came to look at it, and they agreed on a sales price, but she wouldn't take a check, so he went away, presumably to his bank, and came back in a few minutes with all the money in cash. She counted it carefully, which must have taken some time, then she signed the title and let him have the keys."

"Did you get his name?"

"She couldn't remember, but she did remember that he said to her, 'Call me Mac.'"

"Aha!"

"Is that helpful?"

"Yes. Did she put his name on the title?"

"No, she just signed it and handed it to him."

"So he could have written any name on the title."

"Or the name of a Delaware Corporation."

"Did she give you a description?"

"She said he was a big guy, very muscular. He took off his jacket because he was hot, and she was impressed by the muscles in his arms."

"Okay," Stone said, feeling deflated.

"That doesn't help, huh?"

"Not in the least. All I know about Mac is that he once stayed at the West Side YMCA. Actually, that tidbit might be more helpful than I thought," Stone said. "Thanks. And send me your bill." He hung up.

Stone went and sat in the chair beside Joan's desk. "We've got a lead," he said.

"What is it?"

"I think the owner of the station wagon, whose name is MacLean, or just Mac, is the guy you shot in East Hampton."

"That can't be, because he didn't have a car."

"He may have had an accomplice, and my best guess is that it was Eddie Jr. The two of them spent time at the West Side YMCA, and Mac could have bought the car on Eddie's instructions."

"Can you prove either of those contentions?" Joan asked.

"Not yet," Stone said, "but that could also explain why the

extra Mercedes station wagon is parked in your garage. Eddie may have had a remote control that you don't know about."

"But how could he get into the house? I had all the locks changed."

"How did he get into the East Hampton house?"

"Good point. Maybe Mac or Eddie has some lock-picking skills, but the locks in the Manhattan house were changed to the Israeli locks that are unpickable."

"Is there a room on the garage level?"

"Yes, a maid's room, currently not in use."

"Maybe that one eluded the locksmith."

"I'll get Geoffrey to check it out."

"In the meantime, let's assume that Eddie has access to your house."

"You just made my skin crawl," Joan said.

FORTY-THREE

Stone left a third message for Bridget in three days, which he considered his limit on attempts to make contact. Anything after that had the odor of dumpee about it, so he stopped calling. Dino was unavailable, so he went to Clarke's alone. Rush hour was not over, and he and the bartender had to work at maximum reach to get a bourbon into his hand.

"I'm sorry," a woman's voice said, "is my ear crowding your elbow?"

"It was, but now it's working perfectly," Stone said, demonstrating by bringing his glass to his lips. "I'm grateful for the inadvertent assistance of your ear."

"My ear accepts your thanks," she said. "Do you have a name?"

"I do, and it is Stone Barrington."

"That sounds as if it should be carved in limestone on the exterior of a financial institution."

"That is a refreshingly new one," Stone said. "What does your name sound like?"

"Like a place to get a tan."

Stone thought about that. "Help me out here."

"Sandy Beech. Sandra, really, but it doesn't work that way."

"Are you in the profession of guarding lives?"

"I'm in the profession of preserving them."

"You pickle people?"

"That happens only when they have passed from my hands."

"Then you are a physician?"

"I am."

"Do you practice at a nearby institution?"

"At the Morgan Clinic."

"Is that the sort of place where over-imbibers go to dry out?"

"Not necessarily," she replied. "Though that is on our menu of services. We're in the business of whatever ails you."

"That's very broad-minded of you," Stone said.

"It's a third-generation private clinic," she said. "We're still operated by a Dr. Morgan."

"If I may change the subject, have you dined yet this evening?"

"I have not."

"Then will you join me in the dining room for a repast?"

"Thank you, yes. I was just getting hungry when your elbow rose to my rescue."

He led her to the dining room, where the headwaiter gave him his usual table, even though Dino was absent. "I recommend the beef," he said.

"Sold. I'd like my repast medium rare, please."

Stone ordered steaks and a bottle of the Pine Ridge Cabernet.

Sandy tasted it. "Ah, deep and dark," she said.

"My first requirement of a Cabernet is that I be unable to see through it."

She held her glass to the light. "Passed," she said.

As she took her first sip, a man who was not the waiter appeared at her elbow.

"I see you didn't bother to wait," he said.

"Au contraire," she replied. "I waited for an hour. That's the point at which I consider myself stood up."

"Sandy," Stone said, "if you wish to revert to your previous plan, I will try to get over it."

"I do not wish to revert," she replied, taking a larger sip of her wine.

"Then it remains for me to invite your acquaintance to join us," he said. "I can have the waiter bring us another chair. My name is Stone Barrington," he said, extending a hand.

"I'm not interested in your name," the man said, "or another chair. What I'd like is for you to leave, and I'll take your seat."

"Sandy," Stone said, "what is your wish?"

"I wish my acquaintance to dematerialize," she said, "and reconstitute himself somewhere else."

"I think that's very plain," Stone said to the man. "But I'll translate for you: the lady wishes you to go away."

The waiter appeared with their steaks, elbowed the man out of the way, and served them.

"Now," Stone said to the man. "It remains only for you to leave us in peace."

"Perhaps you'd like to step out onto the sidewalk," he said, indicating the side door to the street.

"Oh, Bryce," Sandy said, "really now. I've had enough of you." She made a shooing motion. "Scat."

"Would you like me to translate that?" Stone asked.

"I've issued you an invitation," the man said to Stone.

"Declined," Stone replied. He reached into his coat pocket and produced his NYPD badge. "Would you like the assistance of some gentlemen in blue? There are two parked outside in a police cruiser."

That gave him pause. "Another time," Bryce said, and left.

"His full name is Bryce Newcomb," Sandy said, "in case you'd like to hunt him down and thrash him later."

"I will not devote a single brain cell to remembering that name," Stone replied, "nor an ounce of energy to thrashing him."

"I didn't make you for a cop."

"That's because I got over it some years ago. Now I practice the law instead of enforcing it."

"How remunerative of you."

"I didn't leave the NYPD quietly," Stone said. "They threw me out."

"Was it something you said?"

"Said, and said repeatedly," Stone replied, "but their excuse was a bullet in the knee."

"They shot you?"

"No, I was previously shot, in the line of duty."

"So you are now a pensioned invalid?"

"No, I recovered and am now an attorney-at-law, but I took their pension anyway. It keeps me in bourbon."

"And how did you make this legal leap?"

"I already had the law degree when I enrolled at the police academy, but I still had to pass the bar exam, which I eventually got around to. An old law-school buddy gave me some work, and it ensued that I made partner."

"Was that the end of your professional road?"

"No, after that I made senior partner, so I hardly have to work at all."

"I've noticed that about senior partners in other fields—medicine, for instance. Do you often come to this place alone?"

"No, I usually come with an old friend, who was my partner when we were homicide detectives about two hundred years ago. But now and then he has other demands on his time."

"Before I forget, you shouldn't think that Bryce Newcomb has just gone away."

"He has a vengeful heart, does he?"

"To the extent that he has a heart, yes."

"So I should watch my ass?"

"That puts it very nicely."

"Will my badge cover me?"

"I wouldn't count on it," she said. "He's an unreasonable sort."

"How does he earn his daily bread?"

"He doesn't. An ancestor or two made that unnecessary."

"One of those, huh?"

"I'm afraid so."

"I have a client like that who has turned out to be a lot of trouble. Well, not a client, exactly. I'm his trustee, appointed by his stepmother, whom he is suspected of murdering."

"Are there a lot of suspects?"

"Only one, thus far."

"Well, with two trust-fund babies in your life, I suppose you should *really* watch your ass."

"I'll try to remember that."

FORTY-FOUR

They left the restaurant together.

"Thank you," she said, "perhaps another time?"

"Another time, what?"

"I'll have a drink at your place."

"You anticipate me."

"It saves time."

"May I drop you at your place?"

"Assuming you can get a cab. It's starting to rain, and they don't like getting wet."

Stone lifted a hand, and a taxi screeched to a halt.

"Well done," she said, climbing in. Stone followed her into the cab. She gave the driver her address, and he drove on.

"Your address is in Turtle Bay?"

"Clever of you to figure it out."

"My house has a view of the rear of your house, across the

garden," he said, "so don't bother lowering your blinds." He told her the number.

"What a coincidence," she said.

"Do I detect a note of disbelief?"

"Just a tiny one."

"Let's see, your predecessor in the house worked for a bank, and she was murdered."

She turned and looked at him.

"There's that disbelief again," he said.

"You read the papers, don't you?"

"I do, but as it happens, I was a witness to her murder."

"You were in the house?"

"No, a friend of mine and I were having a drink and waiting for her to start vacuuming her place, when a man walked up behind her and stabbed her with a knife."

"Wait a minute. You said you were waiting for her to start vacuuming?"

"She did that every day at about the same time, and she preferred doing it naked. She was very beautiful, so we sometimes watched. She seemed to enjoy that."

"What did you do after the part about the man with the knife?"

"My friend called it in, and we ran over there as fast as we could. But when we arrived, the killer had fled. There was nothing we could do for her. Except catch her killer, which we eventually did."

"Well, Stone," she said, "you certainly have a vivid imagination."

"Which part of my recitation of the facts do you attribute to my imagination?"

"You said you 'called it in.' How?"

"Well, we didn't want to get put on hold, so my friend, Dino, called the police directly."

"Does he have some sort of personal influence with the NYPD?"

"You might say that. He's the police commissioner of New York City."

"Did you imagine that, too?"

"Tell you what. When you get home, turn on your computer and google the NYPD, and see if the commissioner's name isn't Dino Bacchetti."

"What will happen if I google you?"

"I've no idea. I've never googled myself."

"That shows a refreshing lack of self-involvement."

"You've seen my badge," Stone said. "Here's my business card. Anything else I can do for you?"

"Not on this occasion," she said, handing him her own card. "But we can discuss that another time, if you'd like to call me."

"What are your office hours?"

"Nine to five, unless there's a major flap on."

Stone tucked away the card. "All right, but you must promise, after you've researched me as thoroughly as you like, to always believe everything I say. Nobody likes to be called a liar."

"We'll see," she said. The cab came to a halt at her house.

"In that case, I won't call you," Stone said. "You can call me, if you like. Good evening."

"Would you like to take the shortcut from my back door across the gardens?"

"Thank you, yes." He got out of the cab and followed her to her door, where she stood aside and pointed.

"That way," she said.

"Thank you. And again, good evening." He departed through the back door, walked across the gardens, and let himself into his kitchen. Before he closed the door, he gave her a little wave, and she waved back.

Stone undressed and got into bed. As he did, the phone rang. "Stone Barrington," he said.

"Is this the Stone Barrington with the vivid imagination?" she asked.

"No, this is Stone Barrington, the honest man. What can I do for you?"

"Please accept my apology and call me as soon as you like."

"As you wish. *Bonne nuit.*" He hung up and switched on the TV.

FORTY-FIVE

As the TV came up, Stone saw a familiar edifice, but it took him a moment to place it. Annetta Charles's house, now Joan's. He turned up the sound. ". . . found dead in the living room of the mansion, near where a previous murder occurred. The woman was a housemaid, hired only a few days ago. Police said the murder had been perpetrated on a lower floor of the mansion, then the body was moved upstairs to the living room, where the butler discovered it as he was turning off the lights for the night. She was Eastern European and was in this country on a temporary visa."

Stone's phone rang. "Yes?"

"It's Joan."

"I've got the TV on. Were you harmed?"

"Just frightened," she replied. "She was the first person I hired. An agency sent her over."

"Take some deep breaths."

"After East Hampton, I know the drill, thanks."

"Do you want to stay here tonight? Perhaps a few days?"

"No, I'm not going to let the little creep scare me out of another house."

"Are we thinking of the same little creep? The description seems to apply."

"We are."

"Make sure to ask the police to search every room, every nook and cranny, including the garage. Is the extra Mercedes still there?"

"No, it was gone when I got home."

"Did the locksmith replace the lock on the door of the maid's room off the garage?"

"He did. I had a look at that, and my key worked."

"Did you go inside?"

"No, my nerve failed me at that point. If she'd been left in that room, we still wouldn't have found her."

"Keep listening to your nerve, and sleep with your gun under your pillow. It will be more comforting than it sounds."

"I'll remember that."

"Do you want me to come over and spend the night?"

"Certainly not! What kind of girl do you think I am?"

"The regular kind, I suppose."

"Nevertheless, my .45 will be my only company—it's a relief to have it back."

"As you wish. Call if you need me."

"I think I can handle it." She hung up.

A moment later, the phone rang. "Yes?"

"It's Sandy. Does your intuition extend as far as the Upper East Side?"

"No, but the murder was at my secretary's house."

"Was it she?"

"No, she just called. The butler found the body as he was turning off lights for the night."

"How is it that you have a secretary with what was described on TV as 'one of the largest houses on the Upper East Side'?"

"An aunt left it to her—not long ago. She's barely moved in. Why did you think I might have intuited something about the murder?"

"Well, that's what happened at my house, wasn't it?"

"No, it wasn't. I was a witness to that murder. I didn't intuit it."

"Oh, that's right. I'm sorry. I woke you for nothing."

"You didn't wake me. I was intuiting the murder on local TV news."

"Are you going to have any trouble getting to sleep?"

"None at all."

"Because maybe I could help."

"I'm sorry, but I don't extend that invitation twice on the same night. That would be excessive."

"Well, *I'm* going to have trouble sleeping tonight. Do you want to come over here?"

"Thanks, but I'm all settled in with the TV now. Perhaps another night soon."

"How about tomorrow night?" she asked.

"Does the invitation include dinner?"

"Well, we can order in a pizza or Chinese. I don't cook."

"In that case, let's do it at my house." He gave her the house number. "Come over at about six o'clock. I'll give you a drink, then dinner."

"Are you cooking?"

"No, I employ a full-time cook, and she's much better at it than I am."

"How are we dressing?"

"In as little as we can get away with."

"Hmmm," she said. "See you at sixish."

Dino called. "Dinner tonight?"

"Sorry, I'm booked."

"Aha!"

"It's your fault," Stone said. "You didn't show for dinner last night, so I had to get myself picked up."

"And we all know that is easily accomplished."

"You heard about thc killing at Joan's house?"

"In East Hampton?"

"On the Upper East Side. You're a little slow on the uptake, aren't you? There's a murder on your old stomping ground, and you don't know about it."

"The file just landed on my desk," Dino said. "I'll call you when I've had a look at it." He hung up.

Joan seemed much more herself when she turned up on time for work Monday morning.

"How did you sleep last night?" Stone asked.

"Very well once I tucked the .45 under my pillow. It had a calming effect."

"Have you heard any more from the police?"

"A detective called this morning, just to see if I was all right."

"That's not why he called."

"You think he had something more in mind?"

"Based on my experience as a detective, I do. Calling the next morning was not on his checklist."

"He was kind of cute," she said.

"That's what they used to say about me."

"Uh-oh." She went back to her desk.

FORTY-SIX

Stone was at his desk the following morning when Dino called.

"Good morning," Stone said.

"I read the file. There was a murder the other night at Joan's house."

"Told you as much. Was anybody else hurt?"

"Just the maid. I think Eddie Jr. did it."

"Do you have any evidence to support that contention?"

"Only my long experience as an investigator of homicides."

"And that, as the saying goes, will get you a cup of coffee, if you already have seven bucks in your pocket."

"You are a cynic."

"I still haven't heard any actual evidence from you."

"We both know he did it."

"Don't point that thing at me! What's your next move?"

"My people are already searching every room."

"Did they notice that the extra Mercedes wagon in the garage was gone?"

"That was pointed out to them. It occurs to me that Joan may be in danger."

"Why?"

"Because if she dies intestate, the estate will go to Eddie Jr."

"She is not intestate. She made a new will early on, and the only mention in it of Eddie Jr. is that he be excluded from inheriting any part of it."

"He could be looking for revenge."

"Now *that* is a possibility. Is your supposition a good enough excuse to put a guard on her?"

"My superiors require actual evidence of intent before they'll let me do that."

"Then I'll have to get Mike Freeman's people on the job."

"She can afford it," Dino said.

"Well, I guess I'd better find out how stingy she is."

"Let me know."

They both hung up.

Stone walked out of his office into Joan's and sat down. "I've just been on the phone with Dino, and we agree that you need some personal security."

"Is Dino going to spring for that?"

"No, you are. You're richer than the NYPD."

"So you want me to put my hard-earned money into the pocket of Strategic Services?"

"You didn't earn a cent of it. It was an inheritance."

"Nevertheless."

"You can't enjoy spending it if you're dead."

"You're pointing out the obvious."

"Somebody has to."

"How much is that going to cost?"

"Whatever it costs."

"That's what I thought."

"I'll talk with Mike about that, and he'll have them in place before you get home from work."

"Oh, all right. Tell him to send at least one cute one."

"I'll mention it."

"I have a big bed."

"They're not going to sleep with you. That's another service entirely, and Strategic Services doesn't provide it." He left—before she could make any other suggestions—and called Mike Freeman.

"I've been expecting to hear from you," Mike said.

"How many people is it going to take?" Stone asked.

"Well, I surveyed the house, once, for a party, and I still have the plans. I think what we have to do is seal off a couple of floors for Joan to live on. That will mean two on the stairs, above and below, and one on the elevator. We'll also need two men in the garage and one on the roof. I assume we're expecting some sort of attention from Eddie Jr.?"

"That's a reasonable assumption."

"Does the guy have any athletic abilities I should know about?"

"What sort of abilities?"

"Can he climb the sides of buildings?"

"He's not Spider-Man."

"Is he a dead shot?"

"Well, he's shot two women dead. Does that count?"

"Then I guess either he hits what he aims at, or he just gets close enough."

"I think that's a good guess. Oh, he may have bought a Mercedes station wagon, metallic beige. It was in the garage for at least a few hours, so he probably has a remote for the garage doors."

"We'll replace it and give Joan and her staff new devices."

"Oh," Stone remembered. "The interior and exterior locks have all been replaced with Israeli hardware."

"Then we'll need those keys from Joan. We don't have time to pick those things."

"So I hear."

"What else do you hear?"

"Eddie Sr. may have left some loose hardware, in the form of handguns, lying around. The police are searching the house now. They'll probably find them."

"Let's not count on that," Mike said. "We'll do our own search."

"And Joan is packing her trusty, rusty .45. She used it to take out a home invader in East Hampton and the police returned it to her."

"I've read the file on that. It's my guess that Joan is going to be her own greatest threat to both herself and us."

"You can't go wrong assuming that," Stone agreed. "She has a history of not being afraid to shoot people who invade her space—or mine."

"That's both attractive and scary," Mike said.

"Well put. Why don't you have your chat with her here instead of at her house. She'll be less likely to blow you away."

"I'll be right over," Mike said. "Tell her it will be me ringing the bell and not to shoot."

FORTY-SEVEN

Mike Freeman sat in Stone's office with Joan sitting next to him.

"That's it," Mike said. "And don't worry, I'm giving you the family rate."

"I'm not sure I can afford the family rate," she said.

"Okay, I can just treat you like everybody else and double it."

"I'll take the family rate. When will I be safe?"

"When you get home from work, you'll walk into a safe home."

"I'll be home at six."

"We can do that."

She handed him a clump of keys. "Those are the Israeli ones. They're impossible to duplicate, so don't lose any."

"We can duplicate them," Mike said.

"I paid all that money for keys that can't be duplicated, unless you go to Israel, but you can duplicate them?"

"Let's say that we have a little corner of Israel in our cellar, just for occasions like this."

"Just don't lose any."

"Old money is cheap," Stone said.

"I thought you were new money, Joan," Mike said.

"She is," Stone replied, "but her money is old."

"Let me see your .45," Mike said to her.

Joan reached under her skirt and produced the weapon.

"This is filthy," Mike said, examining it.

"I haven't sent the laundry out yet," Joan replied.

"We'll get you a cleaning kit and show you how to disassemble it."

"I thought guns were self-cleaning."

"You've been watching too many infomercials on TV. Guns aren't like that. If you don't take care of them, they can blow up in your face."

"Bring me a cleaning kit," Joan said, "and put it on my bill."

"We'll throw that in with the family rate."

"Even better."

Mike stood up. "Okay, I'm going over to your house and position my people."

"Can I have my .45 back?"

"Not until we've cleaned it."

"Will I recognize it?"

"Barely," Mike said. He put the gun into his briefcase and left.

At five o'clock, Stone buzzed Joan.

"Yes, sir?"

"Come on, I'll drive you home."

"I can get a cab."

"I want to do the walk-through with you and see what Mike's setup is."

"But then you'll know everything."

"Come on, I promise to stay out of your underwear drawer."

Fred drove them, and as he approached the house, the garage door opened, seemingly of its own volition. Mike was in the garage, talking to some of his people. He introduced them all to Joan, Stone, and Fred.

"Okay, let's take the elevator up to the eighth floor," Mike said. They rode up, and one of Mike's people was in the car with them.

"What's that guy doing in the elevator with us?" Joan whispered to Mike.

"He's making sure there are no intruders on the elevator with us."

"Is he armed?"

"All my people are armed."

"Where's my .45?"

They got off the elevator and Mike picked up her weapon, which was lying on the coffee table. He was about to show her how to disassemble it, but Joan fieldstripped it, worked the action, then reassembled it, reinserted the magazine, and pumped a round into the chamber. "Nice work," she said, flipping on the safety.

Mike handed her a leather box. "And here is your cleaning kit. It should always be cleaned after it's fired."

"I can do that," Joan said.

He handed her a small velvet box. "Open it," he said.

Joan found a locket on a gold chain inside.

"I didn't know you were so sentimental, Mike."

"It's an electronic device."

"You mean like 'I've fallen, and I can't get up'?"

"Better than that. All you do is press it, then say whatever you like. 'Intruder,' for instance, or 'fire in the kitchen.' Like that."

Joan pressed it and said, "I've fallen, and I can't get up."

"Perfect, but don't use that line. My people will think you're kidding."

Joan tried again. "I've fallen, and I can't get up. NO KIDDING!"

"That's better. Pretty, isn't it? We gave you the Cartier model. Wear it at all times."

"In the bathtub, too?"

"Especially in the bathtub. We don't want you to hurt yourself trying to get to it when you need it. Don't worry, it's waterproof."

"Won't it hear the splash?"

"Only if you're wearing it. It charges on a pad at your bedside. Leave it there every night when you go to bed."

He gave her a remote control device. "We've put one of these on all three of your cars, so the garage door will know you're coming. The buttons turn on and off anything you like. Just point it."

Joan pointed it at a lamp and it came on. Then she turned it off again. "Good."

"The button at the bottom turns everything in the house on. When you get into bed for the night, you can turn all the lights off from there."

"What's Geoffrey going to do for a living?"

"Geoffrey is now your driver and bodyguard. He spent the afternoon training on our firing range. He already has a carry license."

"Then who's going to be the butler?"

"Geoffrey, when he's not protecting you."

"You'll get your money's worth out of Geoffrey," Stone said.

They continued their tour until Joan had everything down pat.

"Okay, I'm briefed," she said to Stone. "Now make all these people disappear, so I can take a bath and change. I'm going out for dinner."

"They will seem to disappear, but they'll still be there to protect you," Stone said. "Who are you having dinner with?"

"Eddie Jr.," she said. "Only kidding. It's none of your business."

"Give one of these people his name, so they won't shoot him," Stone said. "Good evening to you!"

"And good riddance to you!"

FORTY-EIGHT

Eddie Charles Jr. sat in the attic over his late father's dressing room, where he had eluded the people who searched the house earlier. He opened the hatch that led to the attic, put a foot on the top of the unit that held his father's trousers, and lowered himself silently to the floor. He had concealed himself just in time, and he had overheard every word of Mike Freeman's briefing with Joan. He could sleep on the bed in the dressing room, to which his father had sometimes been banished by his wife.

He was exactly his father's size. It pleased him that, after years of having been denied the use of his father's clothing, he could now pick and choose from his things. He undressed and got into fresh clothes and a sheepskin coat for the outside weather. He took a hat, a scarf, and some gloves, then slipped out of this shoes and left the dressing room through its rear door, emerging into a hallway that led to the eighth-floor living room. He stopped and stood stock-still for two minutes, listening for movement in the house. He heard nothing.

He padded across the living room, into the study, then through the narrow door that allowed a bartender to reach his workstation. He opened the bar refrigerator and found some canapés left over from Joan's party. He ate them all, washed down with a bottle of beer. He cleaned the plate carefully, dried it, and placed it on the shelf with the other serving dishes, then he wiped down the beer bottle with a damp rag, replaced the cap, and put the empty back into the fridge, behind two rows of full bottles. Finally, he went into his father's study and sat down at his desk. He opened the top right-hand drawer and found it empty, except for innocent office supplies. He closed the drawer and reached down into the well of the desk, where his feet would go, and found a concealed button. He pressed it, causing a tray to eject, which he then pulled all the way out to expose its contents. The tray had not been found by the security people.

It was not as deep as a drawer, but it held a half dozen weapons and their accessories. He picked up a snub-nosed .38 and examined the tip of its barrel. Good. He removed a silencer from its bed and screwed it into the barrel. Then he selected a loaded magazine and shoved it into the weapon's grip and worked the action, moving a round into the chamber, ready for firing. He pocketed four more loaded magazines and a shoulder holster, then he pushed the tray back into the desk until it closed and latched. He put the weapon on safety, then slowly lowered the hammer.

He was about to leave the room when he noticed a leather box on the desktop. He opened it and found that it had held three remote controls, one of which was missing. He had heard the discussion between Freeman and Joan about how to work it. He put one of them in his pocket.

He went back into the bar, opened the large butler's lift, removed two of the wire shelves and stowed them in a cabinet. Then he crawled into the unit, pressed a button, and pulled the door shut. He had done this often when he was a teenager, slipping out of the house when everyone was asleep.

The lift in which he sat stopped in the kitchen, and Eddie very carefully opened the door an inch and listened. Someone was rummaging in the big Sub-Zero refrigerator. He waited until he heard the fridge door close and footsteps cross out of the kitchen, then he got out of the butler's lift and stretched his limbs. He was ready to greet the world now.

He took his shoes in his hand and tiptoed down the service stairs to the main floor of the house, stopping to listen for two minutes. Nothing. He crossed the marble lobby, still without his shoes, and held the little remote control under a table lamp and examined the controls. Finally, he took a deep breath, held it, and pressed the button that read: FRONT. The door quietly opened, and he stepped outside. He closed the door softly behind him, slipped into his shoes, and walked quickly out into the night. He was a free man once again, and he had a home to come back to, if he was careful.

FORTY-NINE

The following morning, Joan came into Stone's office. "Do you have a minute?" she asked.

"Sure. You've never asked before." She looked nervous, he thought.

"I have a problem," she said, "and I don't know what to do about it."

"Tell me."

"I think Eddie Jr. is somewhere in my house."

Stone looked more closely at her. She was a wreck. "But the people from Strategic Services conducted a rigorous search," he said.

"I know. And I know that I sound crazy."

"So, do you have any evidence of his presence?"

"No."

"Have you heard anybody moving around in the middle of the night?"

"No."

"If we're going to order Mike Freeman's people to conduct another search, we'll need to give him a reason."

"I don't have a reason. I just have a feeling that he's there."

"A 'feeling'?"

"That's it. Just a feeling. I want the house searched again, and this time, by different people."

"Listen, you're the boss here. If you want the house searched again, then it will be done. I'll speak to Mike. And if you think of anything else, please let me know."

"If my feeling changes, I will."

Joan left, and Stone called Mike Freeman.

"Yes, Stone?"

"Your client, Joan Robertson, wants the house searched again. As she puts it, she has a 'feeling' that Eddie Jr. is still somewhere in the house, though she has nothing concrete to support her feeling."

Mike was quiet for a moment. "You're serious, aren't you?"

"I am. And she wants a whole new team to conduct the search."

"What is your view of her mental state?"

"She's a very smart lady, and she's got the bit between her teeth about this. Let me suggest that if you find evidence of Eddie's presence in the house, you refund her money for the first search."

"That's fair," Mike said. "I'll have a new team put together, and they'll be at work by, say, one o'clock, and they won't leave until they've pronounced the house Eddie Jr. free."

"Go to it." Stone hung up and called Dino.

"Bacchetti."

"It's Stone. What do you think of Joan's mental state?"

Dino was quiet for a moment. "Why do you ask?"

"You know her well, and I just want your opinion."

"What has caused you to question her sanity?"

"I don't question her sanity. I just want to know if you do."

"Well, now that you mention it, I think we have to consider what she's been through the past few days: two people have been shot dead in her residences. And she shot one of them herself. I think that experience would rattle anybody, even a usually sane person."

"So you think she's usually sane?"

"Certainly."

"Could being 'rattled,' as you put it, cause her to believe things that are not true?"

"Listen, there are a lot of usually sane people who believe that what's-his-name won the last election. Anything is possible. Now, what has caused you to question Joan's sanity?"

"I don't question her sanity. I just want to know whether *you* question her sanity."

"I would never have questioned that, if you hadn't brought it up."

"So it's my fault?"

"What's your fault?"

"That I'm questioning her sanity."

"Well, it's not my fault and there are only two of us in this conversation, so it must be your fault."

"Let me put it to you this way," Stone said. "If Joan still believes that Eddie Jr. is somewhere in the house, after Strategic Services has searched her house again and found no trace of him, is she nuts?"

"Those people of Mike's are very good," Dino said. "My wife is one of them."

"I concur. Nevertheless, after the first search, Joan 'feels' that Eddie is still somewhere in the house."

"How firmly does she believe this?"

"Firmly enough to order Mike Freeman to conduct a second search, this time with a different team."

"Well, it seems to me that one of two things is happening," Dino said.

"What are they?"

"Either one, Eddie Jr. is hiding somewhere in Joan's house, or two, Joan is batshit crazy."

"You mean, not entirely sane."

"Batshit crazy is worse than not entirely sane. It's batshit crazy."

"Thank you for your psychiatric diagnosis," Stone said. "I think that, since a new search has been ordered and should be underway shortly, we should withhold final judgment on the matter of Joan's sanity until such time as we know the results of the new search."

"Tell them to check the washer and dryer," Dino said.

"Why the washer and dryer?"

"Because if Eddie Jr. is living there, he has to have clean socks and underwear at some point."

"I will add that to their instructions," Stone said, then hung up. He texted Mike Dino's order, and Mike responded that his crew was on the way to Joan's house.

FIFTY

A couple of hours later, Joan came into Stone's office. "Will you go over to the house with me? I know that Mike's people are there, but I'm still afraid to go inside, unless you're there and armed."

"I can arrange both of those things," Stone said.

Fred drove up to the garage door at Joan's house and stopped. "We need a new code to get in," he said to Stone.

"Hang on," Joan said. "I've got it." She dug into her purse, came up with the remote control, and pressed the button.

The garage door silently opened, and Fred drove them in. They were greeted by Mike Freeman and his crew leader.

"I'm glad you came," he said. "I've got something to show you."

They followed him up to the kitchen and into the laundry.

"In there," Mike said, pointing at an appliance. He handed Stone a pronged piece of plastic, like big tweezers. "So you won't leave DNA on anything."

Stone opened the door and probed the interior, then came up with something black.

"What's that?" Joan asked.

"A sock," Mike said.

"Well, Dino called it. He said that if someone is living in the house he would need socks and underwear."

"There are boxer shorts, too, and they're Eddie Jr.'s size."

"So he is living here!" Joan said with some satisfaction.

"Not necessarily," Mike said. "Come with me." He led them into what seemed like a small apartment, with a sofa, a TV set, and a bed. Beyond that was a large dressing room, with many suits, jackets, shirts, and shoes on display.

"Wow," Joan said.

Mike opened a dresser drawer and fished out a pair of socks and a pair of boxer shorts. "These are the same size and by the same maker as the socks and underwear in the dryer."

"Were the ones from the dryer damp or hot?"

"They were at the temperature of everything else in this room," Mike said.

"So the things in the dryer could be Eddie Sr.'s, not Junior's?"

"Exactly," Mike said.

Joan spoke up. "Eddie Sr. and Eddie Jr. were the same size and wore the same size of everything."

Mike nodded and continued, "They could have been put in

the dryer before or just after Eddie Sr. died, then forgotten by the maid. But there's still another possibility."

"Not another possibility." Joan sighed.

"Although the things in the dryer are Eddie Sr.'s, Eddie Jr. could have been wearing them, and as recently as today."

"Oh, swell," Joan said.

"Is there any indication that Eddie Jr. might be using this place, either for sleeping or for laundering?"

"Possibly," Mike said. He shone his flashlight at the top of a cabinet holding suits. "There's a trapdoor up there, leading to an unfinished attic."

"Any sign that Eddie Jr. has been there?"

"Absolutely none, but it's the kind of place that a small boy might use when playing."

"Eddie Jr. is not a small boy," Joan said.

"Ah, but he used to be," Mike said. "And so he would certainly remember it."

"Why would there be a bed in this dressing room?" Stone asked.

"Oh, that's right, you're not married," Mike said. "Sometimes married men annoy their wives and get banished from their shared bed. My guess is that, when they renovated this house, Annetta insisted on that bed being available."

"That would have been just like her," Joan said.

"Can the washer or dryer be heard from the master bedroom?" Stone asked.

"No. We turned everything on in the laundry and not a peep got to the bedroom."

"Has the bed in the dressing-room suite been slept in?"

"It doesn't appear to have been used, and it was neatly made up, with fresh linens."

"So, what do we do now?" Joan asked Mike.

"May I make a suggestion?" Stone asked.

"Please do," Mike replied.

"Let's put the socks and underwear back in the dryer, and tomorrow, let's see if they're still there and not back in a drawer."

"We can set a few invisible traps, too," Mike said.

"I don't want Eddie Jr. caught in some kind a of trap," Joan said.

"Not a bear trap kind of trap. This is an old private eye trick: you moisten a hair or a piece of thread and stick it to the door's edge. If somebody goes in or out, the hair falls away, unnoticed, except by our man. Then we'll know if somebody has been in the room."

"I like it," Joan said.

"It has the advantage of not shooting somebody in the head," Stone said. "Can you stand another night in the house, Joan?"

"We can have people on duty all night," Mike said.

"Okay, but not in my bedroom."

"You'll have your alarm locket to use, if the room is breached," Mike said.

"Okay, let's do it," Joan said. "What do I have to do?"

"Nothing," Mike said. "Come home after work, get in bed, watch a movie, or read a book until you're sleepy. If you feel or hear something, don't move, just press the locket."

"Stone, will you sleep in Eddie Sr.'s dressing room?"

"No, we'll want to leave that for Eddie Jr. But there's a lock on the dressing-room door, so you can block the access to the bedroom."

"Good," Joan said. "Let's do it."

FIFTY-ONE

Fred drove Stone and Joan back to his house, and they resumed work, as if nothing had happened. Stone thought it a good time to call Sandy Beech, and he did so.

"Ah," she said. "I was just thinking about you."

"Pleasant thoughts, I hope."

"Oh, yes."

"Dinner tonight? We might discuss those thoughts."

"We might, indeed. See you at six."

At ten minutes past six, Stone's bell rang. He pressed the button and said, "Come in." Then he walked toward the front door as she entered, looking around. "Oh, this is nicer than my house," she said.

Stone led her to the study, poured her a drink, then took her on the ten-cent tour. They returned to the study with empty glasses, and Stone refilled them. "The bedrooms are upstairs. I'll spare you looking at beds." They sat down before a small fire in the hearth.

Stone raised his glass. "To second dates. They're so much more fun than first ones."

She raised her glass. "And to the absence of old boyfriends."

"Have you broken it off with Bryce Newcomb?"

"Yes, but he probably hasn't noticed yet."

"How did you come to know him?"

"I met him at the bar at P. J. Clarke's," she said, laughing. "I thought you'd appreciate that."

"I wish I'd met you first," he replied.

"Oh, so do I. He just becomes more and more of a pest. I wrote him a nice note, suggesting he go fuck himself."

"Do you think he'll get your point?"

"Perhaps not. He can be quite dense at times."

A beep was heard, and a face appeared on the screen that covered the front door.

"Goodness," she said. "You have a video of Bryce?"

"No, that's from a camera, live, pointed at the outside of the front door."

"Did he ring the bell?"

"No."

"It seems he's taken to following me," she said. "I believe that is the last stage of stalking."

Stone thought the last stage of stalking was homicide, but he didn't mention that. "Let's hope so. Would you like me to go out and speak to him?"

"Please don't. He will certainly take a swing at you, and then the police would come, and we'd be late for dinner."

The doorbell rang.

"Oh, no," Sandy said.

Stone pressed a button. "Good evening," he said. "Go away."

"That would take care of most people," Sandy said, "but not Bryce."

Stone looked up to find Fred standing at the door.

"Ms. Beech, Fred Flicker, who is my driver and factotum."

"How do you do, Ms. Beech? Mr. Barrington, would you like me to speak to the gentleman?"

"Thank you, Fred. Try not to hurt him."

Fred disappeared.

"Hurt Bryce? That little man?"

"Don't underestimate Fred."

"I hope he doesn't underestimate Bryce!"

"We'll see," Stone said, pressing another button on the screen that gave them a wider shot from another angle. He turned up the volume a little.

Fred opened the front door. "Good evening," he said. "May I help you?"

"I want to see Stone Barrington," Newcomb said.

"Mr. Barrington is not receiving callers," Fred replied.

"Listen, Shorty," Newcomb said, reaching out and taking Fred's lapels. There was a flurry of motion, then Newcomb was on his knees, and Fred was holding him there by a wrist, which was bent.

"I hope you are receiving me loud and clear," Fred said.

"Otherwise, I shall have to break a bone, and who knows where that could lead?"

"Okay, all right," Newcomb said. "I'll go quietly."

"It would be a mistake for you not to do so," Fred said, releasing the wrist. "Now go, before this takes a turn for the worse."

Newcomb hurried away, holding his wrist. Fred came back inside and closed the door. "I don't think we'll hear from him again this evening," Fred said to the camera.

"Thank you, Fred," Stone said, then sat back and sipped his drink.

"That was impressive," Sandy said.

"And effective," Stone replied. "Fred is an ex–Royal Marine commando."

Fred came to the door. "Cook has asked me to tell you that dinner will be served in this room," he said, wheeling in a tray and setting things on the table behind the sofa, then opening and decanting a bottle of wine.

"Hungry?" Stone asked.

"Ravenous," Sandy replied.

FIFTY-TWO

Eddie Jr. entered the house through the service entrance to the kitchen, tilting a hat over his face to thwart a possible camera. He stood inside the butler's pantry and listened for signs of security people, while he pulled on a pair of latex gloves. He removed his shoes and held them in his hand, as he traversed the kitchen. He went to his father's dressing room and found the door leading to the master bedroom uncharacteristically closed and, by the position of the thumb lock, locked. He liked that, because if anyone tried to enter, they would first have to unlock it, making noise that would alert him.

He emptied his pockets, stripped off the shoulder holster, then hung up his father's overcoat, suit, and tie. He then went to the laundry room, removed his shirt, underwear, and socks, and dropped them into the washing machine. He added a dollop of detergent and switched on the machine. Silently, it began its work.

He thought about using the bed but changed his mind. Instead he took a blanket and pillow from a shelf and stretched out on the sofa, making himself comfortable. After a moment, he got up, went to where he had left his pocket contents, removed the silenced pistol, and returned to his makeshift bed. After a moment of listening for alien sounds, he fell asleep.

He woke before dawn, went to the laundry, and shifted the washed items to the dryer, then he took the iron from its cupboard and lowered the built-in ironing board. By the time he had shaved, bathed, and dressed, the dryer had finished its work and he removed the contents, ironed the shirt and boxers, and folded them carefully. Somewhat to his surprise, he found himself with two pairs of socks and underwear, and he remembered that he had previously left a set in the dryer.

He put away the shirt in its appointed place, folded the socks and shorts, and put them with their mates. Then he took the extra socks and underwear back to the dryer and dropped them inside.

He dressed and let himself quietly out of the house well before eight o'clock, which would be when the security people changed shifts. Then he put on his shoes and walked over to Lexington Avenue where there was a good diner. He ate a hearty breakfast, then he caught a cab to Eleventh Avenue, where most of the car dealerships lived, and browsed the showroom and sales lot of the Mercedes-Benz dealer.

A salesman materialized but didn't crowd him. "May I answer any questions?" he asked gently.

"Tell me about that," Eddie said, pointing.

"That is an E55, three years old, with twenty-two thousand miles on the clock. The engine is from the AMG department, and it is the fastest Mercedes of its time. The color is obsidian black. Would you like to drive it?"

"I would," Eddie said.

The man produced a key and handed it over. "I'll be here when you return. Try not to get arrested."

Eddie got into the car, adjusted the leather seat, started it, listened to the engine for a moment, then drove into the street. He got a hint of what the car could do, then returned it to the lot without getting arrested. The salesman named a price, and Eddie made an offer. He followed the man into the showroom, where he consulted his boss.

"Any financing?" the salesman called from his manager's desk.

"I'll give you a check," Eddie said. "Your bank can call my bank."

After a chat with the dealer's financial person, Eddie signed some documents and asked that they register the car to another Delaware corporation that Eddie had set up. He wrote a check for the full amount and waited ten minutes while the man disappeared and made the requisite phone call to his bank.

Three-quarters of an hour after he had walked onto the lot,

Eddie was driving north on the Henry Hudson Parkway, and after that on the Sawmill River Parkway, which was great sports-car country.

Later in the morning Eddie parked semi-legally on Madison Avenue and went into a Realtor's office to inquire about rental apartments. He couldn't continue sneaking into and out of his father's house, without being shot by a security guard or having to have an annoying conversation with the police. He soon found housing—a cozy, one-bedroom furnished apartment in the East Sixties with a garage in the building. He would make one more visit to his father's house that night and leave with two suitcases full of clothing.

One of the Strategic Services men took his boss into the laundry room and showed him the dryer. "Boxers and socks still there," he said. "No prints."

"So, he hasn't been here?"

"Yes, he has. Let me show you something." He led his chief into the dressing room and pointed at a rack of hanging clothes. "There was a beautiful tan cashmere jacket hanging there yesterday." He knew because he had been thinking of stealing it when the job ended. "Also, some other jackets and suits, plus, shirts and underwear from the dresser. And two large alligator suitcases have been taken. Looks to me like the guy has moved out."

FIFTY-THREE

Stone and Joan sat in Stone's office and listened to Mike Freeman's report. "We've been there six days," he said. "For the first part of that we detected very subtle signs that Eddie Jr. had been sleeping there. He was very careful, until last night."

"Did you catch him?" Joan asked.

"No, but he removed a considerable amount of Eddie Sr.'s clothing and two alligator suitcases, which indicates to us that he's moved out and, likely, won't be back."

Stone pondered that. "Where is Eddie's beige Mercedes station wagon?" he asked.

"Found at an impound lot," Mike replied. "Nobody has claimed it just yet."

"So he needs transportation," Stone said, "and a roof over his head."

"He seems partial to Mercedes," Mike mused. "We'll check the classified ads and the dealers' used car lots."

"Good. If you were footloose in New York, Mike, how would you seek shelter?"

"Well, he's already used two clubs and the YMCA, and the houses of two people he knows—you and Joan. Maybe he's looking for something more permanent, like a furnished apartment. Again, we can check the classified ads, and there are real estate offices up and down the Upper East Side. You've seen them, their windows full of photographs of their properties."

"It's one thing to check the classifieds, but it's another to send people out to search Realtors' shops. That sort of work is more suited to police departments. I mean, I know you can do it, but you have a client who's tight with a buck." He nodded toward Joan.

"What about it, Joan?" Mike asked. "You want us to do a real estate search?"

"I'm tight with a buck," Joan said. "I think we'll hold off until he tries to kill somebody again."

"What if it's you?" Stone asked.

"I'm packing these days," Joan replied. "I think I'd welcome the opportunity to get a shot at him."

"Mike," Stone said, "you didn't hear that."

"Hear what?" Mike replied.

Herb Rice, an investigator for Strategic Services, was assigned the task of identifying cars that Eddie Charles Jr. might have bought. He went quickly over the classified ads, but nothing jumped out at him. He took a cab to the Mercedes dealer on Eleventh Avenue.

As he alit from his cab, Herb saw a dozen or fifteen cars parked in the lot for used—or "pre-owned"—cars, as fancy dealers liked to call them. Maybe half met the criteria for an Eddie Jr. purchase. Through the showroom glass, he could see a single person, probably a salesman, at a desk. He walked inside.

The man rose from his seat. "Good day," he said. "May I help you?"

Herb took his ID card from his wallet and held it close enough for the man to read. "Yes, if you can," Herb said. "I am a licensed investigator with the security firm of Strategic Services."

The man's face registered *Cop, private dick*. His personal experience with such people during two divorce proceedings had not been pleasant.

Herb could see that the man's body language conveyed he was clamming up. Herb smiled as warmly as he could manage. "I wonder if you might have sold an, ah, pre-owned Mercedes to a man named Edwin Charles Jr. in the past couple of days? He's about five-nine, 160 pounds, dark hair, well-dressed." He paused. He was not getting a good reaction, so he said, "Mr. Charles is being sought as part of a murder investigation by the police."

"Is he a suspect?"

"He's a person of interest to the police."

"I haven't sold a car to anyone like that in the last week," the salesman said.

"Pretty quiet around here, isn't it?" Herb asked.

"We've got two salesmen on vacation. I'm holding down the fort. And anyway, we see most of our customers by appointment."

The phone on the man's desk rang. He sat down and picked it up. "Hello? Well, hello, there."

A woman, Herb thought.

The salesman held his hand over the receiver. "Anything else? I've got to take this call."

"No," Herb said, and the man went back to the phone call. Herb knew when he was licked. He walked out and began looking for a cab on the street.

The salesman pressed a button on the phone. "Thanks, Sheila," he said. "The coast is clear." He hung up.

Herb got into a cab and gave the driver an address, then he made a cell phone call. "It's Herb. I've checked the classifieds—nothing there for us. I've just come from the Mercedes dealer. Eddie Jr. might have shopped there, but the only salesman on duty is a cop-hater, and he gave up nothing. Yeah, I'm on the way back now. Hang on, can you check new registrations of used Mercedeses from the last day or two? It's a long shot, but it might give us something." He hung up and zoned out, until he was back at the office, then he went immediately to a colleague's cubicle. "Anything?"

"One new registration of a used Mercedes yesterday.

A three-year-old obsidian black E55, with 22K on the odometer."

"Name of owner?"

The man consulted his notes. "Registered to a Delaware corporation, only a PO box for an address in Wilmington."

"Bingo!" Herb said.

FIFTY-FOUR

Stone hung up the phone and buzzed Joan.

"Yes, sir?"

"Strategic Services just called," he said. "A used Mercedes like mine was registered yesterday to a Delaware corporation. Sounds like Eddie, doesn't it?"

"Was there a street address?" she asked.

"No, just a PO box in Wilmington."

"Oh."

"I had an idea, though, about how to search the furnished apartments classified, without paying Strategic Services to do it."

"Great! How?"

"You do it," Stone said, eliciting a groan. "A thought. Look for apartments with garage space." He hung up. He called Dino.

"Bacchetti."

"It's Stone. Eddie Jr. has got himself some new wheels." He related the details.

"A smart move, looking for apartments with garage space. Eddie wouldn't expose his new ride to the elements, would he? Are Mike's people conducting a search?"

"No, Joan is. She's too cheap to pay Mike. A woman after your own heart."

"Tell her to call me if she comes up with something. I'll have my guys run it down for her."

"You're a prince of a guy."

"Clarke's, six-thirty?"

"Okay." They both hung up.

They were on their first drink at the bar when Stone became aware that someone, reflected in the mirror, was staring at him. "Oh, shit," he said to Dino, sotto voce. "Here's trouble. Check out the mirror."

"Got him," Dino said. "You didn't mention him being that big."

"He is."

"Remember the first rule when dealing with a big guy."

"What's the first rule?"

"Get in the first punch. He'll be easier to deal with if he's flat on his back."

"That would be a good idea if we weren't in Clarke's," Stone said. "If I keep punching guys in here, I'm going to get myself eighty-sixed. Then who are you going to drink with?"

"It's so like you to think of me first," Dino said. "Handle it."

Stone swiveled his stool through a one-eighty. "Something you want to say to me?" he asked Bryce. Sandy's old boyfriend.

The man was caught off guard. "Well, uh . . ."

"That's what I thought," Stone said. "Now, do you want to continue this outside, or do you just want to take a hike?"

Bryce turned and walked out.

"Nicely handled," said Sid, the bartender. "Unless he's waiting for you when you leave."

"Thanks, Sid, you're a sweet guy. Wait here, Dino. I'll be right back."

"No chance of that. I want to watch this."

Stone headed for the back door, while Dino jumped off his stool and followed him.

Stone pulled on a pair of cashmere-lined gloves; no point in getting his knuckles bruised. He walked outside, ready to duck a punch. The block was empty.

"I guess he thought better of it," Dino said.

"Let's get some dinner," Stone said, shucking off his gloves and walking back inside.

The maître d' seated them at their usual table, and they ordered steaks and a bottle of wine.

Stone's phone rang. "Hello?"

"It's Sandy," she said.

"Hi, there."

"Are you still at P.J.'s?" she asked.

"Yes, we're just finishing dinner."

"Be careful how you go. I heard from a friend that Bryce

has rounded up a group of friends and will be waiting for you outside."

"What is it with that guy?"

"I'm a real catch. He hates losing me, and he hates you for managing that."

"Do you know if they're armed?"

"Bryce doesn't carry, but some of his friends do, licenses and everything."

"Got it," Stone said. "Thanks for the warning." He hung up.

"What?" Dino said.

"That was Sandy. She says Bryce and some friends are waiting for us outside."

"What do you mean, *us*?"

"All right, me. Are you bailing?"

"Of course not. Are we ready to leave?"

Stone called the maître d' over. "Would you check outside of the back door and see if there are some guys loitering?"

"Sure." He came back in a minute. "Four of them," he said. "You want to borrow my baseball bat?"

"He won't need it," Dino said. "Thanks, anyway."

The man shrugged and walked away.

"What's your plan?" Stone asked.

Dino was already on the phone. "It's Bacchetti. There are three or four guys hanging around the back door at P. J. Clarke's. I want them braced, searched, and questioned thoroughly. No. No rough stuff, unless they unwisely start it. Call me when you're in place." He hung up.

"I think some rough stuff might be fun to watch," Stone said.

"Do that when you're on your own, and I'll watch," Dino said.

His phone rang again. "Okay, thanks." He hung up. "They're up against the wall," he said. "Let's go."

They walked out the rear door and four men were holding up a wall of the place. They were all dressed in blazers or tweed jackets.

"That's a bunch of pretty shifty-looking guys you got there. Make sure there's nothing in their pockets."

They got into Dino's car and got out of there. "I don't think they'll try that again."

"If they do, I hope you're around," Stone said.

FIFTY-FIVE

Joan came into Stone's office with a sheet of paper in her hand.

"You found the apartment with the garage?" he asked.

"I found four in the East Sixties with garages."

Stone read the list. "It looks like three of them could be with the same garage, and they're all on Sixty-Sixth Street."

"What about the one on Sixty-Seventh Street?"

"It just says 'off-street parking available.' The others just say 'garage.' Fax it to Dino. Let's see what he thinks without hearing our opinion."

"We have an opinion?" Joan asked. "Maybe you could try it on me before you speak to Dino."

"It's one of the three on Sixty-Sixth Street, with garage," Stone said.

"Oh. I'll fax it to him." She left his office.

Ten minutes later she buzzed him. "Dino on one. Can I listen in?"

"Okay, but don't get used to it."

"I mean, this conversation is not going to be about sex, is it?"

"I don't talk about sex on the phone."

"You insinuate things."

"How would you know that, unless you listen in?"

"I'm just saying."

"That's inconclusive."

"Dino is waiting."

Stone picked up. "Hi."

"Which one?" Dino asked.

"We thought we might get your thoughts on that before we expressed a view."

"You're afraid I could be unduly influenced by your opinion?"

"Well, maybe."

"I'm happy to give you my opinion of your opinion," Dino said.

"Oh."

"Well?"

"Our opinion is, it's one of the three on Sixty-Sixth Street."

"That's not an opinion. It's a wild guess."

"Would it put too much strain on your resources to have your officers call at all three apartments?"

"What about the fourth, on East Sixty-Seventh Street?" Dino asked.

"Well, if they have an extra minute."

"I'll call you back."

Another twenty minutes passed before Joan announced Dino was on the phone.

"Hey."

"Hey, yourself. Our opinion is that it's the apartment on East Sixty-Seventh."

Stone took a deep breath and let it out before responding. "What is your reasoning?"

"Our reasoning hardly matters, if East Sixty-Seventh is the one."

"All right," Stone said, trying not to grit his teeth. "Try East Sixty-Seventh."

"How would you proceed?" Dino asked. "If you were in command."

"I'd check the mailboxes."

"Why? You want to read his mail?"

"You're doing this just to annoy me, aren't you?"

"I'm doing it out of logic. Annoying you is the cherry on top."

"Logic dictates that if a mailbox has Eddie's name on it, he lives in that building."

"Oh, not just his car? Don't you think that Eddie could live in one building and park his car in another building?"

"Maybe. I'd sure like to have a couple of NYPD detectives knock on all the doors, though."

"I'll call you back."

Eddie Charles Jr. parked his new/old Mercedes E55 in the garage and walked across the street to his apartment. He checked his mailbox to see if the car's registration certificate had arrived. They had claimed to be short-staffed and promised to mail it. The mailbox was empty. He went back across the street, got into his car, and started it.

Joan buzzed Stone. "Dino on one."

Stone picked up. "Any luck?"

"Yeah, my guys figured out which garage Eddie parks in."

"Is the car parked there now?"

"No, they saw it drive away when they were walking up the block to the garage."

"A pity they weren't a little earlier."

"Well, you can't have everything."

"At least we know he lives on East Sixty-Sixth."

"Yeah, but there's no point in knocking on the door when we know he's not there."

"They could check the mailboxes."

"I'll see if they think that's a good idea. Call you back."

Joan walked in. "Any luck with Dino?"

"No. Dino has apparently devoted his career to getting me to put a bullet in my brain."

"Don't do it."

"I have no intention of doing it."

The phone rang, and Joan picked it up. "Dino?" She handed Stone the phone. "It's Dino."

"Hello there," Stone said.

"Hello, yourself. My guys were checking the mailboxes on East Sixty-Sixth and found one that looked good, but they got a call. A shooting on East Seventy-Second Street. Shootings come first. I'll call you after they've had a chance to open the mailbox."

"Thank you so much. I'll wait with bated breath." He hung up. "Joan, can I borrow your .45 for a minute?"

FIFTY-SIX

Joan sat down in Stone's office. "No," she said.

"No, what?"

"No, you can't borrow my .45 for a minute."

"A minute is long enough."

"I'll tell you what you're always telling me," she said.

"What's that?"

"Take a few deep breaths. You'll feel better."

Stone took a few deep breaths. "You're right, I feel better."

"Now, tell me what to do."

"Dino claims there's a reported shooting on East Seventy-Second, and he's had to pull his men off and send them up there."

"Do you believe him?"

"Sort of. I mean, I wouldn't put it past him to lie about the shooting except I know how bad he wants Eddie Jr., who is his only suspect in the murders of Annetta and the maid."

"What about Mac? Isn't he worried about Mac?"

"No, sweetie. Mac is dead, and Dino doesn't think you're a murderer. In his own mind, he's already cleared the shooting of Mac as self-defense against an armed intruder."

"What about the East Hampton cops?"

"They don't matter. They know that Dino is more credible with the press than they are, so they're not going to argue with him."

Joan shook her head as if to clear it. "I'm sorry, I've forgotten what we're talking about here."

"We're talking about what to do next," Stone said.

"Got it. What are we going to do next?"

"As I see it, we have two choices: one, we can go up to East Sixty-Sixth Street and check all the mailboxes to see if Eddie's name is on any of them, then do the same at the East Sixty-Seventh address."

"What's the second choice?"

"We can sit here calmly until Dino has cleared the East Seventy-Second Street shooting scene, then let him go back and check on the mailboxes."

"He's already found a mailbox with Eddie's name on it. Which one was that?"

"I can't remember. Can you?"

"No."

"Then I think we should use public funds in the form of Dino and his men, instead of wearing ourselves out trooping up and down the East Sixties."

"Which one is likelier to give me a clear shot at Eddie Jr.?" Joan asked.

"Joan, you're not going to get a clear shot at Eddie Jr. Mac was a fluke. If you take another shot at Eddie Jr. and hit him, you're going to live the rest of your life with the consequences of that action hanging over you, and some of those years are likely to be in a women's correctional institution, where you'd have to learn to like girls instead of boys."

"You are such a pessimist!"

"I'm a realist, and you know it. You're going to have to content yourself with seeing Eddie Jr. in prison, not in his grave."

"I like the second one better."

"I know you do, but it won't work."

"Tell you what. Let's drive up to East Sixty-Sixth Street, park, and wait for the cops to get over whatever's happened on East Seventy-Second Street, then go back to work looking for Eddie Jr."

"That's a reasonable suggestion, but only if you give me your .45 for safekeeping."

"You really know how to take the fun out of things," she said.

"Give it up."

She reached into the big purse on the floor beside her chair, fished out the .45, and set it on his desk.

Stone picked it up, popped out the magazine, racked the slide, and released it. He put the racked bullet back into the magazine, then pocketed everything.

"Be nice to it," Joan said.

FIFTY-SEVEN

Edwin Charles Jr. sat at the wheel of his idling Mercedes E55 and watched his father's house. Only the domestic staff appeared to be in residence, and not all of them. The Strategic Services people had gone back to wherever they had come from. He decided to be bold. He took the little remote control that he had stolen from the desk in the study and pressed the "alarm off" button, then he pressed "garage" and put the car into gear.

He drove to the garage door and slowly approached it. The door went up, as it should. He drove in and chose a parking spot for his car. Then he got out, reset the alarm, went to the elevator, and pressed eight. The car rose silently to that floor and the door opened. Eddie held the door back and stepped out of the car. He could hear no sound. He cased the floor thoroughly, finishing up in the study.

Eddie searched the desk drawers and found what he was

looking for: some of his father's stationery, which was too fine and expensive to throw away. Then he took out his father's Montblanc pen, the old-fashioned, fountain kind, and checked the ink reservoir: nearly full.

He opened a drawer, went to the correspondence file, and removed a sheaf of his father's letters, which he often wrote by hand. Eddie and his father had been taught penmanship, by the same ancient tutor, to write in the old-fashioned Palmer Method script. He found several letters his father had written as first drafts before he gave them to his secretary to be typed. The woman had filed the originals as the copies.

Eddie put on some latex gloves, took from his pocket a will that he had written out, then rewrote it on his father's stationery. He went over the result carefully, looking for anomalies and found only two. His father had crossed *T*'s on a slant, and his *R*'s at the ends of words were idiosyncratic. Eddie wrote two further drafts of the will before he found his work to be perfect. He went back through the file of copies until he found two that had been witnessed by household employees, two of them dead and one who had been dismissed, signed on dates shortly before his death. He practiced forging all three until he had them perfectly. Then he wrote the signatures on the will as witnesses. Finally, after more than an hour's work, he took the will into his father's secretary's office and ran it through the Xerox machine. He placed a copy in the correspondence file, then wrote *Last Will & Testament* on the original and sealed it in a matching envelope with a bit of glycerine found in the desk.

He returned everything in the desk to its original position, then placed the envelope in the out tray on the desktop, where someone would eventually find it.

He went to his father's dressing room and began packing still more of the man's clothing into another, smaller piece of his alligator luggage and the matching briefcase.

Stone and Joan sat in the rear seat of Stone's Bentley, with Fred at the wheel.

"What do the cops call this thing we're doing?" Joan asked, yawning. "Whatever it is, it's extremely boring."

"It's called a stakeout," Stone said, "and it's going to be boring until something happens."

"What if nothing happens?" Joan asked.

"Then we will sprout roots and limbs and be here forever."

"I vote not to do that," she said. "I vote to go home. Let's let Dino's people do this. It's what they're paid for."

"I seem to remember suggesting that some hours ago," Stone said.

"Fred," Joan said, ignoring Stone. "Please drive me to my house. I have a remote for the garage, so you can park there."

"Yes, ma'am," Fred said.

"Fred . . . ?"

"Yes, miss," he replied. "Sorry."

"Drive on."

Fred glanced at Stone in his rearview mirror, and Stone nodded almost imperceptibly. Fred put the car in gear and drove away. At Joan's house, she used the remote to open the garage, and they drove in. Nobody noticed the E55 parked at the rear.

Eddie heard a beep and went to look for an alarm screen. Somebody had entered the garage. Then another beep, and the symbol for the elevator lit up. Eddie locked the door from the study to the master bedroom and waited quietly, ready to bolt through the door to the laundry, if necessary.

FIFTY-EIGHT

Joan switched off the alarm with her remote and pressed the eighth-floor button. "Could I talk you into having a drink?" she asked Stone. "A stakeout makes me thirsty."

"Done," Stone said. "A stakeout makes everybody thirsty."

She went into the study, to the bar, and poured them both a Knob Creek. "Joan," he said, "when we were driving away on Sixty-Sixth Street, do you remember a man coming out of the garage and walking up the street?"

"Oddly enough, I do. At first, I thought he was Eddie, but he wasn't."

"Same here," Stone said. "I know him, though. I just can't remember where from. Maybe he was dressed differently than when I saw him before."

"I'll take your word for it."

"It will come to me in a minute," he said.

Joan sat down at the desk and began opening drawers. "I haven't been through this thoroughly since I moved in."

"What's in it?" Stone asked.

"Just the usual crap you'd expect to find in desk drawers," she said. "Hey, wait a minute, there's a shelf or something that isn't quite closed, but I can't budge it. Give me a hand, will you?"

Stone struggled out of his comfortable seat and walked around to her side of the desk. "It looks like a stenographer's shelf, but there's no knob on it." He ran his fingers along the underside of the desktop. "Hang on, there's a button." He pressed it and the shelf sprang open, as if spring-loaded.

"Well, look at that," Joan said, pointing at the array of weapons.

"And one is missing," Stone said. "From the indentation, it could have held a snub-nosed .38."

"That's what our murderer used, isn't it?"

"And what Mac, your dead guy, was carrying."

"Gotta be Eddie," Joan said.

"Bryce something," Stone said.

"What?"

"Bryce Newcomb."

"Don't change the subject."

"That's the name of the guy we saw. Dino and I encountered him at Clarke's. An old boyfriend of Sandy's."

"What on earth are you talking about?"

"It's the name I couldn't remember before. He was the guy leaving the garage."

"So what?" Joan asked. "Tell me that, please."

"He was belligerent. It happened a second time, but Dino called somebody and got him and some companions braced."

"'Braced'? What's that?"

"Put up against a wall and searched. We managed to leave unmolested."

"You don't want to talk about this gun drawer anymore?" She pushed, but nothing happened.

"Press the hidden button again."

Joan bent over and looked along the desktop. "Here it is," she said. "And here's something else." She reached into the bottom level of the out tray and fished out an envelope. They both read it.

"Put it on the desk," Stone said, "and don't touch it again."

"But it says 'Last Will & Testament,'" Joan replied, reaching for it.

Stone slapped her hand. "We need two pairs of latex gloves," he said.

"Sorry, I never carry latex gloves."

"Look in your laundry room and kitchen," Stone said, "and round up two or three members of the staff. We need witnesses."

Joan got up and went to the door that led to Eddie Sr.'s dressing room and the laundry and tried to open it. Locked. She started for the kitchen, to enter the laundry from there, then there was a loud *click*. She went back to the door and tried it again. This time it opened. She returned to Stone. "Give me back my .45," she said. "Somebody's in Eddie Sr.'s dressing room.

"It's in my overcoat pocket, on the back seat of my car."

Joan found the button on the desktop again and opened the shelf containing the firearms. She picked up the officer's .45 and a magazine, shoved in the magazine, then racked the slide and switched on the safety. "Come on," she said.

Stone took his pistol from its shoulder holster and followed her to the door.

Joan stepped back. "You first," she said.

"Gee, thanks." Stone turned the knob. The door opened, and he stepped back. He entered the room the way he had entered rooms when Dino was backing him up. It was empty. He walked into the laundry, then into the kitchen. "Clear!" he shouted.

Joan came into the room. "It wasn't clear a minute ago," she said. "That door was definitely locked, and I definitely heard it unlock."

"Well, he's gone now."

"Eddie Jr.," she said.

"Probably. How do you call the servants together?"

She took out her remote and pressed a button. "That's all hands on deck," she said.

First Geoffrey and then a maid entered the kitchen. "Yes, miss?" Geoffrey said.

"We need two pairs of latex gloves," she said.

Geoffrey went to a drawer, opened it, and produced two pairs of latex gloves. "We use them when dusting the crystal," he said.

Stone put on a pair and handed Joan the other. "Okay,

everybody," he said. "Come look at something in the study." He led them to the desk, where the envelope still lay. He and Joan put away their weapons. "Now," Stone said. "We found this in the out tray on the desk a couple of minutes ago. Joan picked it up, so it will have her fingerprints on it. Note that the writing on the envelope says 'Last Will & Testament.' Have either of you ever seen this before?"

They both shook their heads. "Do you recognize the handwriting?" Stone asked.

"It's in block capitals," Joan said.

"All right," Stone said. "We're going to open the envelope and read the contents, and you two will be witnesses that we found it sealed."

Everyone nodded.

Stone picked up a letter opener from the desktop and slit the envelope without breaking the seal. He removed the single sheet of paper and unfolded it on the desktop.

"I recognize the handwriting," Geoffrey said. "It's Mr. Edwin Sr.'s."

"I'm going to read it aloud," Stone said.

FIFTY-NINE

Stone read the will aloud. It was very similar to what he had dictated for Annetta's will, mentioning some small bequests, except for the last paragraph:

"I do give and bequeath to my wife, Annetta, the remainder of my estate, which, in the event of her death, shall pass in its entirety to my stepniece, Joan Robertson. Should she become deceased after my wife's death, the entire bulk of my estate, including that she inherited from Annetta, shall pass to my son, Edwin Charles Jr., and his descendants."

Stone turned to Joan. "Do you see what that makes you?"

"Lucky?"

"No, a target."

Joan thought about that for a moment. "Oh, shit," she said finally.

"Of course, that's if this will stands up to a great deal of scrutiny. Geoffrey, do you recognize this handwriting?"

"Yes," Geoffrey replied. "It's Mr. Edwin Sr.'s. Not a doubt."

"You know," Joan said to Stone, "before I came to work for you, I worked for a few months as Eddie Sr.'s secretary, while he was looking for someone permanent. I saw his handwriting every day, and that's it."

"It's the Palmer Method," Stone said. "My mother used it, too. She tried to teach it to me, but I didn't have the fine-motor skills to execute it, nor the patience to stick with it."

"Tsk, tsk," Joan said, wagging a finger.

"What does Eddie Jr.'s handwriting look like?"

"I don't recall ever having seen anything he wrote," Joan said. "He wouldn't even send Annetta a postcard from summer camp."

"All right," Stone said. "Thank you, Geoffrey. You two may resume whatever you were doing. We may need your testimony at some later time."

Geoffrey began to leave, taking the maid with him.

"Oh, Geoffrey." Stone called him back in.

"Yes, sir?"

"Do you recognize the handwriting of the three witnesses to the will?"

"No, sir. Two are before my time and are now dead. The other got fired for drinking on the job, and nobody knows where she went." He left the room.

"Now, Joan," Stone said. "You have two very important jobs: one, you have to find some very good samples of Eddie

Jr.'s handwriting, the more recent, the better; two, you have to find some other samples of Eddie Sr.'s handwriting, several of them."

Joan opened a file drawer in the desk and removed a file marked CORRESPONDENCE. "There you go on number two," Joan said. She continued rifling through all the other drawers while Stone read the file she had given him.

"Nothing here," she said. "Let me check in the secretary's office." She got up and went into a small room behind her.

Stone compared the handwriting in Eddie Sr.'s letters to that in the will. He found nothing to make him question the will.

Joan came back with another file. "Bingo! Eddie Sr. kept half a dozen letters that Eddie Jr. wrote him over a period of years, from about age fourteen to twenty-one, all of them begging for money."

Stone read through the file. Eddie Jr., it seemed, had also been schooled in the Palmer Method, though his execution of it was uneven in quality. It did improve, though, as he matured.

Stone called Dino.

"Bacchetti."

"It's Stone."

"No kidding?"

"I need a handwriting expert. Do you know one?"

"Yeah," Dino said. "She was my secretary when I was running the detective squad at the Nineteenth Precinct."

"You had a secretary?"

"When I became a lieutenant and a squad commander—after you left. This girl was so great, she left her job and went to study handwriting with some guy at CCNY."

"Name and phone number, please?"

"The secretary or the guy?"

"The secretary."

"That's good because I don't know the guy. She's Clarissa Onofrio." He gave Stone the number. "What's this about?"

"I've got what may be a fake will on my hands."

"Big Eddie's?"

"Yes."

"He was a sly fox," Dino said. "See ya."

Stone dialed the number.

"Analysis, Inc.," a female voice said.

"May I speak with Clarissa Onofrio?"

"Who's calling?"

"Stone Barrington, of the firm of Woodman & Weld."

"Oh, I know you. You were Dino's buddy."

"Still am," Stone said. "Dino recommended you for a handwriting analysis job."

"It's what I do," she said.

"Where are you located?"

"Lexington and Sixty-Fifth," she said.

He gave her the address of Joan's house.

"What time?"

"Fifteen minutes ago," Stone replied.

"I'll take a cab."

"Add it to your bill."

Clarissa was a classic Italian female, but prettier than most. She looked around her. "This is some place," she said.

"Yes, it is," Stone agreed. "I want to show you a will and some other handwriting samples that might relate to it." He gave her some gloves, but she fished her own from her handbag. "Standard equipment," she said.

He handed her the will.

"Just a second," she said, before looking at it. "Am I defending or attacking this will?"

"Does it matter?"

"It could," she said.

"I just want to know if the guy who wrote it is the same person who wrote these other letters." He handed her Eddie Sr.'s correspondence file.

She switched on the lamp near her chair and read the will. "Very nice," she said. "An excellent example of the Palmer Method."

"Please look at the other letters in this file," Stone said.

She read through half a dozen. "Very interesting," she said.

"I'm glad they're interesting," Stone said. "But did the same man write both the will and these letters?"

"I'll tell you this," she said. "I'd rather defend this will in court than attack it."

Stone's heart sank.

SIXTY

Clarissa held up the will. "That being said, I think this one is bogus."

"Why?" Stone asked.

"I'm still thinking about that," she said.

"Have a look at these," Stone said, handing her Junior's begging letters.

"These are juvenile," she said immediately.

"You haven't even read them yet."

"Oh, all right, if you insist." She read them. "This person wrote the will," she said. "I take it they're by Eddie Sr. as a youngster."

"No, they're by his son, Eddie Jr."

"That does it for me," she said. "Eddie Jr. forged the will."

"Pretend we're in court. Make your case."

"The overall shape of the letters in the will is too wide, by a hair; he picked up on the slanted *T* crosses and the strange

R's, but he would have written this sort of document too carefully to miss that. He would have stuck strictly to the Palmer Method. Eddie Jr.'s letters show excessive care to impress his father. Eddie Sr.'s will is too carefully written. Eddie Sr. would have dashed it off, as he did the letters in his correspondence file."

"If the top five handwriting experts in New York were given the will, how many would say it's a fake?"

"Three," she said. "Four, if I were one of them. The other two are too dense to see the subtleties." She examined her fingernails. "I'm also more persuasive. A smart judge would accept my opinion more readily."

"Write me the best opinion you can produce," Stone said. "Joan will give you a computer and a printer. Address it 'To whom it may concern.'"

When Clarissa was done, Stone handed it to Joan. "Ask Fred to go over to Sixty-Sixth and Sixty-Seventh streets and find Eddie's mailbox. Have him put Clarissa's report inside. I want Eddie to see it."

"Why?" Joan asked.

"Because if we can convince him we're on to his forgery, it will no longer be in his interests to kill you."

"Why don't I do that instead of Fred?"

"Because he might see you before he sees the report and be moved to act immediately."

"Got it," she said. She stuffed the letter into an envelope, addressed it, and went to deliver it to Fred.

Eddie Jr. sat in his car and phoned Bryce Newcomb.

"Yeah?"

"They're gone. Meet me at my place in five."

"Right."

They both hung up and arrived at the building's doorstep simultaneously.

"Let's go make a plan," Eddie said, opening the inside door.

"You've got mail," Bryce said, taking the letter from the mailbox and handing it to him. "Hand delivered, too. No stamp."

Eddie took the envelope and led the way to his apartment. Inside, he tossed his car keys and the envelope on the entrance hall table, then hung up his coat.

Eddie Jr. poured Bryce a drink, and they both sat down. "Now," Eddie said, "you're going to have to do the shooting."

"Why me?" Bryce asked.

"Because everybody in that house knows my face or has seen a photograph of it. Nobody there knows you. While you're doing it, I'll be establishing a stainless-steel alibi."

"And what will that be?" Bryce asked.

"I'll get into a fight at P. J. Clarke's."

Bryce grinned. "What a great idea! You've already got a reputation there. Now give me some motivation."

"Fifty grand. And I'll do the planning, map it out for you. I'm good at that."

"That's right, you are," Bryce said. "A hundred grand."

"Seventy-five, but I'll give you a sweetener. I'll kill Sandy Beech for you."

"Done," Bryce said, offering his hand. "When and where?"

Eddie Jr. shook it. "That remains to be seen."

"Aren't you going to open the mysterious letter?"

Eddie picked up a legal pad and began to make notes. "Later. First, I have to plan two murders."

SIXTY-ONE

Eddie had drawn an excellent floor plan of his father's house, and he taught it to Bryce, room by room, switch by switch. He gave Bryce the little remote control for the entire house and showed him how to operate its various features. "Pay attention," Eddie said. "There's going to be a quiz." Bryce paid attention and passed the quiz handily.

"Now," Eddie said. "Show me how Sandy's place looks."

"Hers is simple," Bryce said. "First of all, it's right behind Barrington's."

"No kidding?" Eddie asked.

"Small world, huh? New place, previous tenant died. Ground floor, so it's easy for you to get to. A turn in the hallway makes for good cover." He drew a picture for Eddie.

"Is she a wary person?"

"Not in the least. She'll answer the door on the first ring, so be ready."

"Is there an intercom?" Eddie asked.

"Yes, but it's connected to the street doorbell. Ring that, and she'll respond. Tell her you're delivering a gift from Cartier, and you need a signature, for security purposes. That will bring her to her door at a trot. When she answers, shoot her in the head, no delay. Then close the door and walk out. Go down to Third Avenue and take a cab. Get out at the Ralph Lauren store, go in the side door and out the front door. Take another cab to P. J. Clarke's and do your thing at the bar. Take your time. Have you got a piece?"

"I'll use this," Eddie said, showing him the .38 snub-nosed, wrapped in a dish towel.

"Your prints on it?" Bryce asked.

"It's been wiped clean, the bullets, too. I've got some latex gloves. Here's a pair for you." He reached into another pocket and produced a .22 automatic. "This shooter is for you, Bryce."

"Kind of light, isn't it?"

"It's perfect for close work. Shoot Joan twice in the head. It's what the pros use. Remember to police your brass."

"What?"

"Pick up your spent shell casings and take them with you. Toss the gun and the brass into a dumpster somewhere—before you take off your gloves."

"Got it."

"Okay, listen up now. Let me tell you how it goes with Joan." Eddie took him, on the map, through the entry into the house, pointing at which buttons to push on the remote control. "She'll be on the eighth floor, in either the bedroom or the study—the study most likely. It's where the bar is."

"She have a boyfriend?"

"No, nobody regular. If she surprises you with a companion, you'll just have to shoot them both. There are six rounds in the pistol and one up the spout. Turn your cell phone completely off before you go in and don't turn it on again until you're clear of the neighborhood. When you are, call me, and we'll compare notes."

"Who goes first?" Bryce asked.

"I do. I need to get out and to P.J.'s immediately. You wait until eight o'clock to go into the house," Eddie said. "I'll already be at P.J.'s by then, and Sandy will be dead before I get there."

SIXTY-TWO

Sandy got out of a cab on the corner near her apartment and hoofed the last half block, clutching two large bags of groceries to her breast. Down the block she saw a man loitering across the street from her building. He looked familiar in a not-so-good way, but she couldn't remember his name.

She set her groceries on a wrought-iron fence top and rested for a moment, waiting for developments. The man saw her waiting but didn't come any closer. It was Eddie what's-his-name. He was a usual at Clarke's and a friend of Bryce's. She didn't like him. What was he doing by her building? She hefted her groceries again and started walking toward her building.

Bryce Newcomb found the service entrance, walked to the door, took out the remote control, and pressed the button that turned off the alarm system. He let himself in and, treading softly in his sneakers, made his way to the service elevator, encountering no one.

He got off at the eighth floor, stopped, and listened. He heard someone moving in the study, but no conversation. Joan was alone. Perfect. He pulled on his latex gloves and removed the .22 automatic from his pocket, then examined the chamber. Fully loaded. He moved slowly through the kitchen and laundry, then stopped at the door to the living room. He could see across a sofa toward the study, where Joan was opening and closing drawers and dumping some things into a wastebasket. Bryce cocked the pistol and took a couple of steps into the living room. He wasn't masked, but that didn't make any difference, since the only person who could identify him would be dead in seconds. He held the pistol in readiness and moved slowly past the sofa toward the desk where Joan sat.

Eddie stood across the street and waited for the woman with the groceries to go inside her building. He didn't want witnesses, and he wasn't going to shoot her in the street, creating a fuss. He leaned out and surveyed the street. He didn't see her, but he heard a door slam in the building.

Sandy made it into her apartment, closed the door behind her, and leaned against it, taking deep breaths. Finally, she took the groceries into the kitchen and set them on the counter.

The outside doorbell rang. She went to the panel. "Yes?"

"Delivery from Cartier," a male voice said. "It's a gift. I need a signature for security."

"Come in," she said, pressing the button to release the front door. Then she went to her rolltop desk, opened a tiny drawer, and extracted a gift from her father, who worried about her. The apartment doorbell rang, and she checked the peephole. That guy, Eddie, stood there, holding a small pistol pointed at the door.

"Just a minute," she said.

"No hurry, take your time."

She cocked the derringer pistol, a relic from the Old West, which had over-and-under barrels. To fire the first round, her father had instructed, she was to pull the trigger halfway; to fire the second, pull the trigger all the way. She held the tiny pistol, with its two .45-caliber cartridges, out in front of her, reached down, grasped the doorknob, and opened the door.

Joan looked up and saw the man coming. Her hand was already on the button, and she pressed it. The steno shelf sprang open, and she got a hand on the Government .380.

"This will all be over in a minute," Bryce said, "and then I'll leave you in peace."

"As in 'rest in peace'?" Joan asked, racking the slide and thumbing down the safety.

Sandy held out the derringer and pulled the trigger all the way back. The weapon seemed to explode in her hand, and her hearing went blank, then, as if in slow motion, Eddie left his feet and floated backward, the pistol in his hand firing into the ceiling.

Joan fired a round as she raised the .380 and a red splotch appeared on his chest. Then, to her surprise, the man's face exploded, and he didn't have a nose anymore. She fired again as he fell, just to be sure.

Stone Barrington, who had been sitting on the sofa, got up and took the man's right ankle and felt for a pulse, then shook his head.

"Who the fuck is that?" Joan asked.

"No facial characteristics evident," Stone replied. "Call 911."

"Is it Eddie?"

"Could be. We'll let the police tell us. Call 911 *now.*"

Sandy sat in an armchair, gulping deep breaths, wiggling her fingers in her ears. The noise had been horrific. She yawned, then held her nose and blew. Nothing. Then gradually she began to hear things—a car door closing in the street, a bird tweeting in the back garden. She picked up the telephone and called 911. On the seventh ring, a woman answered, "911 operator. What is your emergency?"

"Uh, ah . . ." What to call it?

"What is your emergency?"

"Dead person, shot."

"Are you all right? Are you safe?"

"Oh, yes. Now there's no threat at all." She gave the woman her address, then hung up.

Stone called Dino.

"Bacchetti."

"It's Stone. I'd like to report a shooting."

"Did you call 911?"

"Joan did."

"That's two shooting calls on the East Side, inside of sixty seconds. Has war broken out up there?"

"Sort of," Stone said. "I'm at Joan's house."

"Who did the shooting?"

"Both of us."

"Is it Eddie Jr.?"

"I don't think so. The corpse doesn't have a whole face, but he's wearing sneakers. Eddie Jr. would never do that."

He hung up and sat down to wait.

END

January 25, 2022

Key West, Florida

AUTHOR'S NOTE

I am happy to hear from readers, but you should know that if you write to me in care of my publisher, three to six months will pass before I receive your letter, and when it finally arrives it will be one among many, and I will not be able to reply.

However, if you have access to the Internet, you may visit my website at www.stuartwoods.com, where there is a button for sending me e-mail. So far, I have been able to reply to all my e-mail, and I will continue to try to do so.

If you send me an e-mail and do not receive a reply, it is probably because you are among an alarming number of people who have entered their e-mail address incorrectly in their mail software. I have many of my replies returned as undeliverable.

Remember: e-mail, reply; snail mail, no reply.

When you e-mail, please do not send attachments, as I never open these. They can take twenty minutes to download, and they often contain viruses.

Please do not place me on your mailing lists for funny stories, prayers, political causes, charitable fund-raising, petitions, or sentimental claptrap. I get enough of that from people I already know. Generally speaking, when I get e-mail addressed to a large number of people, I immediately delete it without reading it.

Please do not send me your ideas for a book, as I have a policy of writing only what I myself invent. If you send me story ideas, I will immediately delete them without reading them. If you have a good idea for a book, write it yourself, but I will not be able to advise you on how to get it published. Buy a copy of *Writer's Market* at any bookstore; that will tell you how.

Anyone with a request concerning events or appearances may e-mail it to me or send it to: Putnam Publicity Department, Penguin Random House LLC, 1745 Broadway, New York, NY 10019.

Those ambitious folk who wish to buy film, dramatic, or television rights to my books should contact Matthew Snyder, Creative Artists Agency, 2000 Avenue of the Stars, Los Angeles, CA 90067.

Those who wish to make offers for rights of a literary nature should contact Anne Sibbald, Janklow & Nesbit, 285 Madison Avene, 21st Floor, New York, NY 10017. (Note: This is not an invitation for you to send her your manuscript or to solicit her to be your agent.)

If you want to know if I will be signing books in your city, please visit my website, www.stuartwoods.com, where the tour schedule will be published a month or so in advance. If you wish me to do a book signing in your locality, ask your favorite bookseller to contact his Penguin Random House representative or the Putnam publicity department with the request.

If you find typographical or editorial errors in my book and feel an irresistible urge to tell someone, please write to Gabriella Mongelli at Penguin Random House's address above. Do not e-mail your discoveries to me, as I will already have learned about them from others.

A list of my published works appears in the front of this book and on my website. All the novels are still in print in paperback and can be found at or ordered from any bookstore. If you wish to obtain hardcover copies of earlier novels or of the two nonfiction books, a good used-book store or one of the online bookstores can help you find them. Otherwise, you will have to go to a great many garage sales.